Hot For Teacher

MONIQUE FISHER

Content Warning

Brief mention of child abuse. The sex scenes in this book are spicy.

Hot For Teacher

One

LATRICE

atrice wakes up at 6:30 on the dot. Her brain has long been wired to wake her up at that exact time during all of summer break. From 6:30 until 7:30 a.m. is her quiet, contemplative time. Theoretically at least. She lies in bed and stares at the ceiling, thinking about her to-do list for the day. She has a consultation at nine, meets with Rachel at noon, then has dinner with Nadia tonight.

Just as she's contemplating whether she has time for a mani-pedi, her phone buzzes. She turns and glares at it like it's her archenemy. Irritation bubbles up inside her. Latrice picks up her phone and sees it's Mark, her ex-husband, and the irritation spills over.

"Fuck me," she grumbles. Latrice considers not answering, but that will just lead to Mark calling back until she answers.

It's the last week of summer break, and Labor Day is

on Monday. Mark has been calling nonstop with all kinds of last-minute questions for her.

Latrice's brother, Thad, is taking her and Mark's son Quincy to Joshua Tree. Quincy starts third grade soon and Mark promised to take him to Catalina, but he, of course, had to cancel last minute for some bullshit reason—which has been the norm since their divorce four years ago. The last time Mark pulled this shit was because his wife, Acacia, insisted he take their twins, a boy and girl named Jelani and Leticia, on the father-son trip he planned for him and Quincy. Mark and Acacia got into a huge fight about him taking the twins which resulted in Mark canceling the trip altogether, leaving Quincy heartbroken and Latrice pissed. But like the hero he is, her little brother came through and took Quincy to Vegas. Latrice wasn't thrilled with the location choice of their trip, but Quincy had a ball. She's grateful he has a reliable male role model in his life; she knows how important that is. Latrice and her siblings all have an amazing relationship with their own dad.

Quincy even talked about taking over Thad's barbershops when he's older, much to Mark's chagrin. Latrice smiles at the thought of those two goofballs having fun and bonding before Quincy starts school.

"Hello, Mark." Latrice answers the phone, trying her best not to sound annoyed. Reminding herself that he's Quincy's father and she needs to keep her cool. Even though Mark is a trifling piece of work and his wife can be aggravating as fuck, Latrice still thinks that it's important Quincy has a relationship with his dad and younger siblings.

"Latrice," Mark replies simply. No greeting, just her name.

Ugh! She hates it when he does this shit.

Motherfucker, you called me. I shouldn't have to carry the damn conversation. Should've just let your Black ass go to voicemail.

He acts like she should just know what it is he wants without saying a word. It's one of the many reasons why they divorced. His selfishness and wandering dick were the others.

"How can I help you?" Latrice rolls her eyes.

"You can help me by getting rid of that bite in your tone, then you can put my son on the phone."

Is this fool serious?

"He's asleep, Mark."

"Well then, wake him up," he orders.

"Acacia may say 'how high' when you tell her to jump, but I don't. So I suggest you watch how you talk to me," Latrice snaps.

Mark lets out an exasperated sigh. "Fine. I'm sorry. Could you please wake up my son ...?"

"You didn't make him by yourself, Markus."

"*Our* son and let me talk to him?"

"Quince doesn't need to wake up for another thirty minutes. You can't wait to talk to him then?"

Mark lets out a sigh. "Look, the twins are in year two of their 'terrible twos' and Acacia's hounding me about spending more time at home, I'm feeling really over-whelmed. And since I'm wide awake, I wanted to talk to the one family member I have that actually likes me."

Latrice rolls her eyes.

Typical Mark.

When he can't get his way by bullying, he resorts to playing the victim. God forbid he actually does some self-reflection and figure out why—aside from his parents—Quincy is the only family member who is nice to him.

"What about Drea?" Latrice asks, knowing the answer but wanting to be petty.

"My sister likes you more than me, and you know it."

Latrice chuckles at the memory of Drea slapping Mark after Latrice caught him with Acacia.

"That's true. Alright look, Thad won't be here until eight. If you want to come by and see Quincy before he leaves, you can."

"I do have a job, Latrice. And other responsibilities. I can't just stop by with little to no notice. You can't just dump that on me."

This motherfucker! Ugh.

She should have known... she should have known better than to actually treat him like a human being. Whenever she tries to show Mark the least bit of decency, this is how he responds. Latrice chalks her naive response to her having just woken up.

"Fine, then wait until he comes back from his trip to talk to him. Goodbye, Mark," Latrice spits, ending the call before he can reply.

She sees it's time to get Quincy up and heads to his room. When Latrice gets there, he's already awake and texting his best friend, Eli. She looks around his room, pleased that he cleaned it. Constantly reminding an eight-year-old to do his chores can get tiresome but when she sees a freshly made bed, a newly vacuumed floor and books stacked neatly on his shelves, it makes having to repeat herself daily almost worth it. Almost.

Quincy looks up at his mom and smiles. He's such a sweet kid, a little cutie. He inherited Latrice's rich, dark brown skin. His features, though, are all Mark's, and as annoying as he is, Mark is an incredibly handsome man. Quincy inherited his amazing bone structure, sparkling brown eyes and dazzling smile. Quincy's neck-length dreads are fresh and stylish. Latrice took him to Thad's barbershop for a retwist and a line up a couple of days ago. Quincy came to Latrice when he was six and asked if he could grow his hair out and get dreads like Uncle Thad. She is adamant that Quincy have pride in his Blackness and was more than happy to ask Thad if he could do it. Mark, of course, was not pleased. 'Mister Corporate' thought Quincy would stand out among the other kids at his school. He neglected to factor in that Quincy's school, Glen Oak Elementary, has a student body of four hundred children, with seventy percent of them being white. Quincy was going to stand out anyway.

Latrice takes his phone. Quincy looks up scrunching his eyebrows.

"Time to get ready. Your uncle will be here soon."

His eyes light up, and he immediately gets his stuff ready.

Latrice places his phone on the bed. "Your dad called earlier."

"If it was to apologize for canceling again, then I'm good," Quincy says, forlorn.

Latrice could kill Mark. He's constantly disappointing this boy. Before he knows it, Quincy will be grown and heading to college, and he won't want anything to do with him.

"The last time we talked, he tried to convince me to spend half of winter break with him and Acacia," Quincy continues. "I haven't decided yet. She still keeps trying to get me to call her 'mom,' by the way."

"Is that right?" Latrice asks.

Latrice is going to have to remind Acacia about boundaries. At first, Acacia thought that she "won" Markus. *She didn't win shit.* He rebounded and married her in a move that Latrice knows was meant to make her jealous. It backfired big-time. Now he's stuck with a woman who was only meant to be a side chick, and he's anchored with two kids by her. Acacia knows this and uses the delusion of winning to ease the pain. While Latrice pities her, they aren't friends. Not even close. Acacia can think herself the victor all she wants when it comes to Markus, but she is not going to disrespect Latrice. Period. She makes a mental note to talk to Mark about his annoying-ass wife. Again.

Latrice and Quincy sit down for breakfast. She made scrambled eggs, bacon and toast. They eat in silence for a bit.

"Are you excited to meet your new teacher next week?" Latrice asks.

"A little. I read the newsletter, and she looks nice."

"Hopefully she will be. Remember to be as respectful to her as you would have been to Mrs. Magrady."

"I will, Mom."

Thad arrives and Latrice opens the door for him before he can open it himself. He is a big man with an equally big heart. Thad has dark brown skin and deep dimples, which he and Latrice inherited from their mom. He's six foot five, with long dreads, and he looks like a linebacker from living at the gym. He's gotten his fair share of attention from the single moms at Quincy's school, but he doesn't go there for Quincy's sake. Besides, Latrice knows he has a thing for Drea even if he won't admit it.

"Hey T!" Latrice smiles.

"Tricey!" Thad hugs Latrice tightly. He walks in and sniffs the air. "I smell bacon. You got any extra?"

"I don't."

Thad looks disappointed. She loves messing with him. She walks over to the kitchen and picks up something covered in parchment paper.

"But," she continues, "I did make you a bacon and cheese sammich. No egg."

She hands it to him. Thad grins like he just won the lottery.

"Yes! Thanks, Trice. Oh, when you get to the boutique can you tell Drea I said she's wrong?"

"Wrong about what?"

"She'll know. It's an inside joke we have going on."

"You two are ridiculous."

Those two fools like each other. A lot. But aside from some flirting and their silly jokes, neither of them has made their feelings known, no matter how much Latrice tries to push them to.

Quincy comes out dressed and ready to go with his luggage, which he promptly drops to hug Thad.

"Uncle Thad!"

Thad snatches Quincy and lifts him up, making sure to not drop his sandwich.

"Q! The man of the hour. You ready to hit the road?"

"Yes!" Quincy beams as Thad puts him down.

"You two have fun. Quincy, call me and your dad when you arrive at the cabin."

Thad picks up Quincy's bags. "Don't worry, sis. I'll remind him, and tell your ex-husband to stop blowing my phone up. That fool acts like this is my first time taking Q somewhere."

"I'll talk to him."

Mark needs to watch his step. Thad may be a fun-loving guy who's a big softie, but he doesn't play about anyone disrespecting him. He let Mark know that before. Sounds like he may need a reminder.

Latrice hugs both her boys, then waves them off as Thad drives away. She feels mixed emotions. She's happy Quincy is getting his trip and she has some time to herself, but she misses him already.

~

Latrice walks into Mtindo and greets Drea and Ingrid. Ingrid hands her a cup of coffee with a smile. Her dark brown hair is styled in loose ringlets, and her copper colored skin is glowing. Latrice has told her more than once how much she resembles a young Lena Horne. Ingrid has on the official uniform of the store, high-end fashion. Latrice's motto is, if they're going to sell high-end clothes, then they have to look the part. Both ladies are definitely playing their role. Ingrid has on a black jersey pencil skirt with a silver-studded chiffon top, both courtesy of Prada. And Drea is wearing black slacks from Armani and a billowy lavender blouse from Arias New York.

Ingrid is the part-time sales associate for the boutique. She's a peach, and currently studying fashion design and business at the Fashion Institute of Los Angeles, even though she looks like a model who would fit in on any runway.

"Quincy's off with Thad?" she asks.

"Yep." Latrice smiles at Ingrid before turning her attention to Drea. "By the way, when he came to pick up Quincy, he told me to tell you that you're wrong."

Drea actually giggles like a schoolgirl. Latrice looks at her with a raised eyebrow and Drea quickly pivots.

"Those two are going to have so much fun," she remarks.

Latrice sips her coffee deciding to let Drea off the hook and not tease her for sounding like a fourteen-year-old, a few seconds ago.

"Take a look at the pictures Thad sent me already."

Latrice takes out her phone and shows them the pics of Thad and Quincy, acting a fool, and making silly faces in Thad's Range Rover. All three ladies laugh.

"Quincy just keeps getting more handsome and Thad is such a sweetheart." Drea smiles.

Latrice notices her scoping the picture closely and running her fingers over the image of Thad. Drea's brown eyes dance as she, no doubt, peeps Thad's deep dimples and Latrice just can't let it slide.

"You see something you like, Drea?" Latrice teases.

Drea looks up. "Huh, what? Oh... no."

Drea looks like she just got caught with her hand in the cookie jar. She plays with her micro box braids—which are styled beautifully in a half fish tail-half down look—before running her hands down her slacks to regain her composure. These two need to quit this tired-ass will they, won't they crap and just date already.

"Wow, you could not be more transparent." Latrice giggles. "I don't know why you two..."

"Yes, you do, Trice," Drea cuts in.

"I'm sorry. I'm lost. Care to fill me in?" Ingrid's brown eyes are filled with wonder.

"Thad and Drea like each other. Like, a lot. A lot, a lot. But Drea has this ridiculous idea that if they date and it doesn't work out, it will make things awkward for me," Latrice explains.

"I'm your best friend, and he's your brother. And your son is our shared nephew. I don't want to put you in a situation where you have to choose which one of us to invite to a family gathering."

"I'd invite you both and trust that you'd be mature enough to be around each other." Latrice sips her coffee.

"Whatever. I don't want to talk about this anymore."

Latrice and Ingrid exchange grins and giggles.

"Hush you two," Drea commands.

She gets saved by the bell when Latrice's nine o'clock appointment arrives. Socialite and heiress Brenda Daniels-Quintero punches in the code and breezes into the boutique.

"Tricey." Brenda smiles. She gives Latrice air kisses on each cheek. Latrice returns the favor.

Brenda repeats this action with Drea and Ingrid. She takes a seat, and Ingrid gets her a glass of sparkling water.

"Sweetie, do you have any Dom?" Brenda asks Ingrid.

"Dom? As in Perignon? Girl, it's nine o'clock in the morning," Drea teases.

"I know, but I'm getting ready to meet mommy and daddy for breakfast at the club and I'd like to be a little buzzed. They are still hounding me and Dame about having a baby."

"Geez, when are they going to let that go?" Latrice asks as she hands Brenda a glass of champagne.

"Your guess is as good as mine." Brenda downs the drink in one gulp. "Now show me this wardrobe you have for me."

"Ah, now this, Ms. Brenda, will make you the envy of all the rich bitches," Latrice gloats.

"Babe, I already am." Brenda smiles brightly.

Ingrid brings out a rack of clothes. Dresses, skirts, shoes, belts, the works. When Brenda said she wanted to update her wardrobe for her new body, and in time for Paris Fashion week, Latrice got to work. First, she got Brenda's measurements, then contacted designers, making sure everything was ready by the deadline. Brenda was in the Caymans with her husband during the summer. That gave Latrice until September to deliver. Every single designer that she contacted responded.

Granted Latrice could hire an assistant easily to do a lot of what she does, and, for the most part, she does have Ingrid do a large amount of the work, like picking up the clothes and making sure they're pressed and hung up. But the one-on-one contact with the clients and designers, she insists on doing it herself. It makes the clients feel special that the co-owner is giving them personal attention. Drea, on the other hand, handles all the financial duties. She likes to joke that Latrice works with the egos, while she works with the dinero.

Brenda takes off her shades and looks at the clothes like she's a kid in a candy store.

"You like?" Latrice grins.

"I *love*. Latrice, you have truly outdone yourself."

Brenda tries on every piece of clothing and takes selfies, some of which include Latrice, Drea and Ingrid. After a couple more glasses of champagne, she bids them all adieu. She says her assistant will come by to pick up the clothes later that day.

Latrice checks her watch. It's half past eleven. She grabs her keys and heads out to meet Rachel.

She walks down the aisle of Target to get some last-minute back-to-school stuff for Quincy as she waits for Rachel. She sent Latrice a text letting her know she was running late.

"Hey, Latrice," Rachel calls out.

Latrice turns around and smiles. Rachel is Eli's mom and the one mom friend from Glen Oak that Latrice has. They have a tradition of sorts where they go shopping before school starts together. They've done it ever since both their kids were in kindergarten.

Rachel MacArthur is one of the popular moms at Glen Oak. But unlike a lot of them, she's not a Regina George type. Latrice tries to avoid all the weird politics of the parental version of *Mean Girls*. Thankfully, because Rachel and Latrice are so well-liked, nobody tends to fuck with them.

Rachel is as sweet as she is pretty. With her shoulder-length brown hair and ocean-blue eyes, she's basically a

Zooey Deschanel lookalike. She and Latrice first bonded over their mutual break ups. They both were going through divorces at the same time and leaned on each other for support. Rachel has been a member of Latrice's crew ever since. Unlike Latrice, Rachel managed to snag herself a second husband in the form of Timothy, a firefighter she met when Eli was six.

"Hey, Rach. How are you?"

"Looking forward to Tuesday. I swear, Eli ate us out of house and home all summer, and whenever he had friends over... my god."

"Who are you telling? Those kids eat like NFL players. I hope Quincy wasn't too much trouble."

"Of course not. Quincy was a doll. He was the only one who was respectful enough to ask for a snack. The rest of those monsters have no manners at all. Especially Dana Kopel's kid. It's a wonder that little shit has any friends at all."

"Well, like mother, like son."

"Got that right."

The two ladies fill their baskets with household items before they head over to the grocery section to buy snacks.

Latrice's phone buzzes. It's Nadia, her and Thad's younger sister.

NADIA

Hope you're ready to get fucked up and slutted out

Latrice laughs out loud. Rachel looks at her and Latrice shows her the text. Rachel laughs as she puts a bag of chips in her basket.

Of course, Rachel, like anyone who has met Nadia, isn't surprised. Latrice's sister is a whole-ass fool. She has taken it upon herself to get Latrice laid. It *has* been a minute. Between her business and raising Quincy, she hasn't had much time for dating. She used to date casually, but the men would always get too attached and she'd have to end it.

Nadia, on the other hand, is a player. Plain and simple. She gets in, gets what she wants and gets out. She's been trying to get Latrice to do the same. Being the eldest of the three Richardson siblings, Latrice has always been the steadfast, good girl. Thad is the light-hearted, fun one and Nadia's the lovable rebel.

LATRICE

I'm ready for a good meal and the company of my favorite baby-sister

NADIA

Awww! You're so sweet. Seriously though, I'm getting you some dick tonight, Trice.

LATRICE

Long, deep negro spiritual sigh 😌

Nadia calls. Latrice answers, but before she can say anything, Nay Nay announces, "The only thing long and deep is the dick we gon' get you. Have your trifling ass at Cork & Marble at seven."

An older Black woman hears Nadia's loud-ass voice and looks at Latrice with disapproval. Latrice gives her a sheepish smile while Rachel tries to hold in her laughter.

"Shameful," the older Black woman chastises as she pushes her cart away.

"Nay Nay, I'm in a damn Target," Latrice says under her breath.

"Then get me off speaker."

"You ain't on speaker, heifer. You're just loud as hell."

Lowering her voice, Nadia asks, "Seriously though, Trice. When was the last time you got laid?"

Latrice thinks back to Carter. He was the last man she dated, and that was a year ago. He was handsome, intelligent, kind and generous, but he—like the others—wanted forever. She wasn't ready. Hell, she hadn't even told Quincy about him or any of them. Honestly, Latrice doesn't know if she'll ever not be scared of pursuing a real relationship.

"It was Carter," Rachel chimes in.

Latrice looks over to see Rachel on her phone.

"When did you hop on this call?" Latrice asks.

"A minute ago. You were too busy overthinking your last dalliance," Rachel jokes.

"I was not overthinking," Latrice argues.

"That's all you do," Nadia interjects.

"You're the queen of overthinking," Rachel says.

Both ladies reply at the same time.

Latrice rolls her eyes. "Whatever."

"For real though, Trice. The beauty of what I'm proposing is that you don't have to overthink anything, and neither does whoever you end up fucking. It's purely a physical thing. You get in, get what you want and get out."

Latrice considers Nadia's proposal. This is basically a truncated version of what she was doing with Carter. And Grant. And Yasir. And Trey. The only difference is she actually dated them. But she mainly kept it physical. Latrice worries she might be out of her depth. Fucking a man on the same night she meets him isn't something she has ever done. While she isn't interested in dating anyone, she also isn't too keen on using anyone either. That's one reason she stopped dating altogether. She was having a tough time looking at herself in the mirror whenever the time came to cut any of those guys loose.

"You're overthinking again, aren't you?" Nadia disrupts Latrice's thoughts.

"No, I'm not." Latrice aimlessly grabs a box of cereal.

"She is," Rachel tattles. "She has that overwhelmed look on her face."

"Judas!" Latrice accuses Rachel, while she simply smiles and blows Latrice a kiss.

"Stop overthinking. It's just sex. Now promise me you'll bring your ass to the restaurant with an open mind." Nadia says.

Latrice lets out an exasperated sigh. "Fine."

"Great! See you tonight. Smooches."

Nadia hangs up before Latrice can reply.

Rachel puts her arm around her shoulder. "Don't worry, Trice. Just relax and have fun. I'm just sorry I won't be at the restaurant with you gals. But I am expecting a play-by-play of the whole evening."

"That's if anything happens."

"It will."

"And what makes you so sure, Ms. MacArthur?"

"I just have great instincts about these things."

Latrice gives her friend a warm smile as they head to check out. As apprehensive as she is about this whole plan, a small part of her—okay, not a small part, more like forty percent—is actually excited to find out if Rachel is right.

Two

LATRICE

Latrice arrives at Cork & Marble just before seven. It's a swanky downtown steak house known for its exceptional wine list and their divine cuts of meat.

This evening proved to be exceptionally windy for early September, so when Latrice jogs from her car to the restaurant, she immediately goes to the ladies' room to check her hair. The lighting at the vanity is definitely working for her. Her skin is glowing. She smiles, showing off her dimples and pearly white teeth. Her curly hair is styled in an updo, with strands of hair framing her face on each side. Her lips are glossy, with a hint of brown color to them. She has on a black spaghetti strap dress that hugs her voluptuous figure and highlights her best assets, namely her ass and breasts. Finding everything in working order, she leaves the ladies' room and immediately spots Nadia. Her little sister always stands out. Her hair is cut short in a fade, courtesy of Thad. She's wearing a forest green low-cut top with a black skirt. Nadia sees her and smiles widely. They hug tightly to greet each other.

"We look damn good." Nadia takes out her phone and they take a selfie. "I'll send this to mom."

"She's going to love it. You'd swear we don't see her every week the way she's always asking us for pics." Latrice laughs.

"You know how proud she is of us. She can't help it, and who can blame her?" Nadia winks.

"I know that's right." Latrice chuckles.

After they take a series of pictures and pick the best one, Nadia sends it to their mom, who responds within seconds.

MOM

Look at my beautiful girls. Have a great time tonight. Love you both! <3

Latrice is grateful she has always been close to her family. Her parents and siblings mean everything to her. She is aware of how blessed she is. Drea didn't win big in the family arena. She and Mark are not close. At all. And that was before she slapped him. Their parents basically pitted them against each other from the time they were kids. Mark was the golden child, and Drea had to fight to get any attention. Latrice can't imagine having an upbringing like that.

"Now, baby sis, I need you to tell me how you scored

us reservations at Cork & Marble. Cause '*I gots my ways. Tricey*' is not going to fly. This place has a mile long wait list."

"One of my clients is an investor, and considering that he walked away with a house, two cars, a vacation home and the dog, he was feeling a little generous when I made the call."

The sisters share a laugh. Nadia is a divorce attorney with her own private practice. And Ms. Thang has connections all over LA. She's able to get the best of everything on short notice: tables at restaurants, box seats at concerts, sporting events, you name it. She's taken Quincy to his fair share of Lakers' games since he was two.

"You heard from Thad and Quince?" Nadia asks.

"Yep. Thad sent me pictures an hour ago, and we talked. They made it to the cabin safely and were headed to get food themselves when I called."

"All I can say is, thank God for our brother because Mark is a worthless piece of shit," Nadia spits.

"Here, here." Latrice taps Nadia's water glass with her own.

"Is Quincy excited for school?"

"Well, he's excited to be starting third grade, but he's not so thrilled about not sleeping in on weekdays anymore."

"Shit, he's eight. He doesn't know how good he's got it. I can't even remember the last time I slept in on a weekday."

"Listen." Latrice shakes her head, and Nadia laughs. Latrice continues, "His new teacher seems great too. Her name is Stephanie Parker."

"Cool. Let me guess? Another white woman?"

"You already know."

"I swear to God that school is allergic to dudes and people of color," Nadia jokes.

Nay Nay's not wrong. Most of the teachers at Glen Oak are white ladies. Mrs. Cora Magrady was one of them. She taught third grade for forty years and retired last May at the end of the school year. The school had a hell of a time finding her replacement. Ms. Parker made the cut, and her hiring was announced in the school newsletter in mid-July. Latrice is sure Principal Tanaka is pleased with her and the school board's choice. The parents and kids will meet Ms. Parker at the welcome back-to-school soiree on Friday.

Nadia looks closely at Latrice's dress. "On to more pressing matters, I'm guessing from the dress that you're game for the dick finding mission?" Nadia asks.

The waitress greets them and asks for their drink orders. Latrice orders a negroni, her favorite cocktail. Nadia orders a dirty martini with an olive.

"I'm leaning into it."

"Finally!"

"Shut up, Nay Nay." Latrice rolls her eyes and chuckles.

Nadia dips her fingers in her water glass and flicks water at her.

"You shut up. So is the man trap you're wearing from Mtindo?"

"No way. There's no chance in hell I'd take something from there. Then I'd have to tell Drea about this cockamamie plan before I'm ready to."

"Well, wherever you got it from, it's perfect." Nadia whistles.

Latrice rolls her eyes playfully. "Hopefully, it's perfect enough to attract the right man."

"I think it already has."

Latrice turns to where Nadia is looking and sees the most gorgeous man sitting at a table near them looking right at her. He looks like a Black Clark Kent. He's even wearing wire-rimmed glasses. There's a quiet power to him that makes Latrice temporarily speechless. He has on a plaid button-down collared shirt, with a dark tie and dark brown khaki pants, but he gives off huge big dick energy, making Latrice picture him in an expensive designer suit. He gives her a sexy smile. *Sweet Jesus, now that's a smile.* His hair is cut in a short taper fade, with small waves on top and a clean line up. *His cut looks fresh, so he must have gotten it done today. Probably for his date.* His build is strong and muscular. *Definitely a gym rat.* His brown skin is clean and blemish free. Latrice spies his low-cut beard and wonders how it would feel against her skin.

Latrice looks back at Nadia. "Holy hell."

She sips her negroni and takes another look. She didn't expect to attract someone so quickly. Make no mistake, Latrice doesn't think she's unattractive by any means. The Richardsons are a good-looking bunch. Her, Nay Nay and T, all get attention from all genders. Latrice just thought she'd meet someone at whatever club Nadia dragged her to, but this man seems to be a contender right from the jump.

"He's fine as shit, Trice, and he ain't with anyone. Do something." Nadia sips her drink.

Latrice turns her attention back to her sister. "Like what?"

"Wink, smile, something. Let him see those dimples. Oh, I know, lick your lips. Do it real slow and seductive like."

"I am not doing that. That's some shit you'd see in a porno."

"Exactly! Do something before he thinks you're not interested."

Latrice looks back over at the handsome stranger. He's checking his phone.

"He's not even looking at me anymore. I probably missed my window."

"*Pffffft*. The hell." Nadia looks over at him. "Hey!"

He and a few other diners look up. The pianist in the corner stops playing. The handsome man is mid-stand and was clearly on his way to the men's room. Latrice covers her face, completely mortified.

"Nadia, what the fuck is wrong with you?" Latrice stares daggers at her sister.

"I wasn't talking to any of you, just him." Nadia

ignores Latrice and points at the handsome stranger. He points to himself, and Nadia nods at him.

She turns her attention to the pianist. "Play something."

The pianist plays *Moonlight Sonata* by Beethoven. The other diners return to their meals and individual conversations. Nadia gestures for him to come over with her finger.

He looks a little embarrassed but comes over anyway. "Hello. You wanted to talk to me?" he asks.

The timbre of his voice is strong, but his tone is apprehensive. Latrice can't blame him after that shit Nay Nay pulled. He had every right to blow her off and walk away. No matter how much she hopes he doesn't.

"Hi, I'm Nadia, and the woman you've been staring at is Latrice."

He looks at them and offers a shy, sexy smile. "It's nice to meet you both."

"And you are?" Nadia asks.

"Nathan. Nathan Woodson."

"Well, Mr. Nathan Woodson, it's nice to meet you as well. Have a seat and join us."

"I'd love to but..."

Here we go. Welp, it was nice looking at him while it lasted.

Latrice feels a twinge in her chest. She doesn't even know why she feels this way. He's just one man. If she decides to truly dive in to this whole one-night stand thing, getting attached is a liability. So why does she want him to stay so badly?

"… I need to go to the men's room first."

The men's room? Of course, he was on his way there when Nay Nay bellowed at him. He's not leaving. Latrice can't help herself and gives him a sweet smile.

He clears his throat and smiles back as he heads to the restroom.

Latrice waits until she sees him walk inside before she goes in on Nadia.

"Seriously, what the fuck is wrong with you? You're so determined to get me laid, and yet, you almost fucked that up," Latrice says angrily in a low voice.

"What are you talking about? That man would definitely be down to blow your back out. And why are you talking so low?"

"One of us fucking has to. It's okay to speak at a normal volume, Nadia. Lots of people do it."

"You should know by now, I'm the exception." She winks.

Latrice is unmoved. "Whatever. The only way I'm going to find out if your back blowing theory is correct is if you ain't here. Now go."

"I will, but first, I want to ask him a few questions."

"Nay Nay, I swear." Latrice summons some patience.

"Don't worry, I'll be cool. And by the way, when I leave this booth, I'm still going to stay close."

"Obviously."

Nathan comes back and takes a seat next to Latrice. His scent invades her nostrils. It's a fresh, clean smell, with notes of citrus. Her nipples perk, and her mouth is suddenly dry. She takes a sip of her drink. *Fuck, I'm nervous as hell.* At first, she was pleased that Nadia got them a secluded booth, but now that Nathan's joined them, she's a little rattled.

"Here by yourself, Nathan?" Nadia asks.

"Looks that way. I had a date scheduled, but it's been half an hour and I haven't heard back from her."

"Her loss will be my sister's gain."

Nathan looks at Latrice and gives her a kind grin. The gin has taken its effect. Between the alcohol, his sweet smell, killer smile, her hard nipples and wet pussy, her inhibitions have been lowered, making her feel a little bold. She looks right back at him and licks her lips slowly. Nathan looks like he's about to jizz in his pants. He lets out a breath while Nadia grins with approval as she scoots out of the booth.

"Okay, I did have a few more questions but I'm going to leave you two." Nadia scoots out of the booth.

"You're not joining us for dinner?" Nathan asks.

"Nope. I'm not a blocker. My sister hasn't been satisfied by a man in a minute, Nathan. So, make this worth her while."

Latrice's sudden boldness evaporates and is replaced quickly with anger and embarrassment. "You literally said you'd be cool." Latrice looks at Nathan. "I am so sorry."

Nathan smirks. "Um, it's okay. Just wasn't expecting her to be so abrupt."

"Seriously, man. Do you not remember how I got you over here?" Nadia asks.

"Touché," Nathan says. "And you have nothing to worry about. Your sister's in good hands."

Nathan looks at Latrice and winks confidently, taking her hand and kissing it. The feel of his soft lips makes her pussy throb uncontrollably. She stifles a moan. Nathan's doing a damn good job of making her feel more at ease. Even so, she needs more courage for this night to go well. She waves the waitress over and orders another negroni.

"I must say, I like the conviction. Just one second." Nadia pulls out her phone and takes a picture of Nathan. "If my sister ends up missing, the police will be the least of your worries. You dig?"

"I understand." Nathan nods.

"Good. Now, if you two will excuse me, there's a fine man at the bar I'm taking home with me. Have fun." Nadia winks.

She saunters over to a fine-ass bald man wearing an expensive suit and nursing a martini. She slides up next to him and says something that makes him laugh.

"Your sister is really something," Nathan says.

"That she is," Latrice responds, shaking her head at Nay Nay's crazy ass. "Again, I'm sorry for her...everything."

"Don't apologize," he replies. "Her *everything* is the

reason I'm sitting here. I'm not sorry. You shouldn't be either."

His voice is filled with a warmth that makes Latrice feel all gooey inside. They look at each other, and time stops. Latrice doesn't know why, but being around him makes her feel desired in a way she hasn't felt in years.

"You're the older sibling of the two of you," Nathan says. It's a statement, not a question.

"I am. I'm the oldest of three. Two girls, one boy."

"Youngest of two. Both boys." Nathan smiles.

"Are you spoiled and always getting your way?"

"I wouldn't go that far. But my brother would agree to that assessment."

"How would you describe it?"

"Basically, it's switched. I'm the one our mother depends on while he gets away with the bare minimum."

"Oof. Sorry. But that is awfully sweet that you look after your mother."

"I try my best. And no need to apologize, it's all good. On to more pressing matters. How long has it been since you were satisfied, Latrice?" Nathan asks as he scoots closer.

"It's been about a year." Latrice rubs her leg against his.

Nathan looks at her in disbelief. "How?"

"Life's complications made pursuing a relationship impossible. Casual or otherwise."

"That's a shame. A woman as beautiful as you shouldn't have any complications when it comes to getting a man into her bed." Nathan gives her a penetrating stare.

"I'm also very selective." Latrice gazes back into his eyes and bites her lip.

Okay, so now that the second negroni has hit, I am not reluctant to do this anymore. Latrice is really enjoying herself. Either that or she's tipsy. Regardless, she's absolutely looking forward to burying Nathan's face between her legs.

"As you should be. I'm very honored to have been selected." His face gets closer.

"As *you* should be," she teases. This earns her another sexy grin. "When is the last time you were intimate with a woman?"

"It's been some time. My date tonight was my attempt to—"

"Get laid?"

Yep, I am definitely feeling this liquor. Who is this brazen woman?

"I'm not going to lie. I was hoping sex would be on the table with her, but, mainly, it was my attempt to try and get out of my shell."

"You do seem a bit shy, but it's sweet."

"Thank you. I wish it was just shyness, but it's a bit more complicated than that."

Latrice wants to ask him what he means, but this whole don't get attached thing is already off the rails. She needs to get it together. This man is not her boyfriend. They are going to fuck, and that's it. She gets them back on track.

"Well, in case it wasn't clear, fucking is definitely on the table with me." Her voice drips with seduction.

Latrice scoots closer to Nathan, rubbing his inner thigh. His muscles are hard and taut.

He lets out a groan before clearing his throat. "Looks that way."

The waitress comes by to take their order. Latrice orders a club soda, having had enough liquor, and Nathan orders one too.

"I'll be right back with your drinks," she replies and walks away.

Latrice's hand grazes between Nathan's thighs. His dick is like steel. She massages his erection.

"Goddamn." Nathan's eyes are closed.

Minutes later, the waitress returns with their drinks. "Are you ready to order dinner? Or perhaps an appetizer?" she asks.

"Could we have more time to look over the menu?" Latrice requests.

"Of course. Let me know when you're ready," she replies, and leaves to help another couple.

Latrice goes back to massaging his increasingly hard dick.

Accepting her boldness with some of his own, Nathan's hand is now underneath her dress, his thumb slowly stroking her swollen clit through her panties.

"How exactly do you want to do this?" he asks.

Latrice closes her eyes and tries to contain the moan

building in her throat. "I don't know. I've never slept with a stranger before."

"I have." His voice is now huskier.

"I'm not surprised." Latrice opens her eyes and gives him a mischievous grin.

"Why do you say that?" Nathan kisses her shoulder, making her wonder why she didn't bring an extra pair of panties.

"I imagine someone as handsome and sexy as you are probably has women lined up around the block begging you to make them come." Latrice's face is flushed.

Holy shit! Did I really just say that? She must have because Nathan grins at her like he's ready to pounce. Latrice hides her embarrassment by looking at her lap.

"I'm sorry—" she begins.

"Don't be." Nathan smiles. "Thank you. You're making my dick so hard I can barely think."

"I am?"

"Hell yeah. Truth is, you've been making it hard since you walked in here."

Latrice slows down her rubbing. Nathan lets out a gentle moan and looks at her longingly. She breathes heavily, her breasts rising and falling. Nathan's eyes travel to her tits while he strokes her clit even more.

"Oh my God." Latrice relishes the sensations jolting through her body.

Just as she feels her orgasm building, the waitress returns. "Have we decided on anything to eat yet?"

Latrice looks at Nathan. "Did you want to stay and

have dinner, Nathan? Or would you like to get out of here?"

By now, they're both breathing heavily and looking like they're going to fuck right in that booth. It's a safe bet what his answer will be, but it couldn't hurt to ask.

Three

NATHAN

Like *your fine ass even has to ask.*

Nathan hands his credit card to the waitress. "We'll take the check, please. Thank you."

"Okay." She takes his card and heads to the bar to close out their tab.

"I feel like we wasted that poor girl's time by not eating anything," Latrice says, catching her breath.

Her skin is glowing and obviously flushed. *She was close to getting hers.* He's even more determined to get her out of here so they can finish what they started.

"Don't worry, I'll leave her a really good tip." He smiles.

Latrice sips her club soda. Her thick lips wrap around the straw, making Nathan think about how they're going to feel around his dick. He's not sure how his evening took this turn, but he's damn happy it did. He had to pull some strings—which involved asking a favor of his brother Leon—to get a reservation here, only for his date to stand him up. Now he's about to fuck this unbelievably gorgeous woman, thanks to her equally beautiful and audacious sister. His head is spinning at the divine luck he's been given. When Latrice first walked in, he couldn't take his eyes off her. Dark brown skin that looks as soft as silk, a body that could make a grown man weep in gratitude and a face fit for a Nubian goddess, all accentuated by those sexy-ass dimples. Nathan was captivated on sight.

He watched her ample ass and wide hips sway as she went to the ladies' room. Watched her tits bounce as she walked to her and Nadia's table. He got hard as a rock.

When Nadia called him over, he wasn't sure who she was talking to. Once he realized it was him, he had to will his heart to stop pounding. After he excused himself and went to the men's room, he called his boy Ronnie. They've known each other since high school when Ronnie was Nathan's only friend. Hell, he still is. Being a foster kid who bounced around a lot, he tended to be socially awkward, and still struggles with it. It took some time before Nathan was comfortable making friends. He and Ronnie have the type of relationship where months can go by and they don't talk, but the minute they do, it's like no time has passed.

The phone ring twice before he answers. "What's up, Nate? How's the date going?"

"She never showed up, but I think I'm being asked to join a threesome."

"With two women?"

"Yes."

"Then why the fuck are you on the phone with me? Go do it."

"Ron, I'm feeling anxious, man."

"Calm down. I'm assuming they initiated it, right?"

"Of course."

"Then take an edible and chill. Enjoy yourself. I'm expecting a full report tomorrow too, my nigga."

"I already took an edible earlier."

"Then take half of one. Breathe in through your nose and out through your mouth a few times. You got this! Nate, man, you keep letting this awkward shit take over, and it leaves you struggling. You got to stop that shit. Tell me, who was the cat that got Aisha Garrett to date him when she turned down every nigga at our school?"

"I did."

"Okay, just go out there do what you did back then."

"These women are a million times more fine than Aisha."

"Word?"

"Yes."

"Yeah, dawg. You going to have to take a whole edible, maybe two."

Nathan took Ronnie's advice, the breathing not the edibles. He didn't want to get paranoid. When it became clear the ladies beckoning him were sisters and it was Latrice checking him out, he could have done a backflip. No offense to Nadia, but her aggressiveness threw him off. And now he's sitting next to this sex bomb while they feel each other up. God, Allah, Buddha, somebody is looking out for him tonight. He makes a mental note to put a little extra in the collection plate when he takes Momma Ernie to church on Sunday.

"I have to say, as much as I've been looking forward to dining at Cork & Marble, I'd much rather eat your pussy." Nathan peppers kisses along her face.

He decided to take Latrice's lead and be direct. So far, she's enjoying it.

The waitress comes back and settles the bill with them and, as promised, Nathan leaves her a nice gratuity. So nice that she smiles widely as she wishes them a lovely evening.

He turns his attention back to Latrice, their faces now only inches apart.

Latrice brushes her hand across his cheek. "There's a Park-Barrington Hotel not that far from here. Shall we?"

"After you."

"Kiss me first."

Say less.

Nathan kisses the shit out of her. His tongue caresses hers as she lets out a needy moan. He tastes the negroni and the sweet gloss from her lips. Both are spellbinding. When they stop, they breathe in sync. Nathan's jaw ticks. He's ready to fuck this woman into a coma.

"Let's go," she says softly.

Nathan kisses her again, then nods in agreement.

Twenty minutes later, he hands his credit card to the

front desk clerk. They quickly get a room key and are in the deluxe suite at the hotel seconds later.

Nathan followed Latrice in his car. The whole ride he kept thinking Leon was going to call him and say, "Gotcha!" His brother has been known to give him a hard time and enjoys fucking with him.

He takes a seat on the king size bed while Latrice grabs them two waters from the hotel fridge.

She sits next to him and lets down her hair, kicking off her shoes.

Nathan pulls her onto his lap and runs his fingers across her face. She lets out a sigh and wiggles her ass against him. This causes more blood to rush to his dick, making him light-headed. He grips her waist for stability.

Latrice leans back and presses her lips against his ear. "Unzip my dress, Nathan."

"With pleasure." Nathan turns her face and gives her another deep, passionate kiss.

He unzips her dress and pulls it down by the straps. His dick throbs with anticipation. *Fuck, she feels good. Her scent—vanilla and honey—is absolutely intoxicating.* He licks her neck and runs his fingers through her natural, curly locks. Latrice unsnaps her strapless bra and Nathan squeezes her breasts while kissing her slowly down her back. She stands and removes the rest of her clothes, turns and looks at Nathan like he's lunch.

"You like what you see?" she purrs.

"Hell, yes," Nathan chokes out. He looks at her like she's a sculpture come to life.

"To hot, wild butt naked sex with a stranger," Latrice announces, lifting her water bottle and grinning from ear to ear.

"I'll drink to that." Nathan stares at her in awe.

They both take sips of water. Nathan then promptly takes off his clothes. He smiles at Latrice's reaction to his naked body. Her eyes look like they're about to pop out of her head, and she bites her lip so hard he's scared she might take a chunk off.

Nathan joins her underneath the covers. The two of them run their hands all over each other's body. His senses are so overwhelmed, he's afraid that if he doesn't get inside of her now, he'll nut before they can even get started.

"So, Mr. Woodson, since you're the expert, how does a one-night stand go?" Latrice gives him a long, delicious kiss before he can reply.

Nathan wills his dick to calm down. "Whew, you made me forget what I was going to say," he replies in a daze.

Latrice laughs and gives him some soft pecks on the lips.

"Mmmm, I wouldn't call myself an expert, but I did have a few in college. To answer your question though, Ms. ...?"

She kisses him again.

"Richardson," Latrice answers.

"Well then, Ms. Richardson, we have an amazing night where I make you come so hard your legs don't work. We spend the night together, then we go our separate ways. How does that sound to you?" He wraps his hands around her waist and squeezes.

"The coming until my legs don't work part sounds like heaven," Latrice purrs.

"It will be." He smiles.

This woman is making him feel things he hasn't felt since... ever. None of the one-night stands he had in college or his actual girlfriends made him feel this confident. At first, he was just matching Latrice's energy, but now he's fully in the zone. It wasn't just the breathing that got him here, it's her. Latrice's touch, her laughter, her smile, her scent. All of it has worked wonders on him. No woman has ever calmed him while enticing him. He loves it and wants more.

They kiss again. He could kiss her forever, unable to get enough of her lips. Nathan gets on top of Latrice, not breaking the kiss. She hungrily kisses him back. Both are eager and aroused. Nathan's head is swimming even more. He rubs his large, strong hands all over her, each of them moaning with pleasure. His lips make their way to her neck, and he gives her gentle bites.

"Nathan." Latrice moans eagerly. "Please fuck me."

"Don't worry, sweetheart. I will, but first I have to taste every inch of this body."

Nathan lowers himself, kissing Latrice's collarbone and her chest. When he's facing her breasts, he takes out his tongue, licking her nipples one after the other. He grabs ahold of one breast and sucks her nipple before popping it out of his mouth and repeating the action with the other breast.

"Ohhh. Nathan," Latrice moans, gripping the back of his head.

He kisses her down her stomach, tracing his tongue around her belly button. She squirms and giggles. When he gets to her pussy, he opens her legs and stares. He's seen some pretty pussies over the years, but this one can only be described as stunning.

"Latrice." He says her name with a heavy breath.

Her pussy throbs, wetness slowly sliding down her folds.

"Fuck me," he whispers.

Nathan eats her pussy like it's his last meal.

"Fuck, Nathan! Fuck." Latrice pushes his head deeper. He sucks her clit and moans, devouring Latrice's ripe fruit. Her juices run down his chin. After ten minutes, he lifts his head up and wipes his mouth.

"You taste so fucking good, Lala."

"Sir, did you just give me a nickname?" Latrice asks, lifting an eyebrow as she looks down at him.

"Yes. You like it?"

"I do."

Yes!

That was a gamble he's happy paid off.

He continues to run his tongue over her pussy. Again and again. His plan tonight is to give this woman everything she's been missing. It's a fucking crime that whatever issues life threw at her left Latrice without someone devoted to satisfying her every need all the time.

"Fuck me, Nathan! Fuck me now!" Latrice screams.

He grabs his pants from the floor and takes out a condom before climbing back on top of her. He rolls it onto his dick and pushes himself deep inside of her. She nuzzles his neck and lets out a shuddering breath.

He turns her head to gaze at her. "You are absolutely stunning."

"Thank you." She smiles.

Her deep dimples make his dick throb. Her pussy constricts around him, and he damn near comes. Nathan kisses her dimples and forces himself to concentrate on her pleasure.

His thrusts are slow at first. As he escalates his speed, her moans get louder and more frantic. She matches his rhythm. He responds by gripping her thighs and rotating his hips. Nathan doesn't just want to make Latrice come first, he wants to make her scream.

Her hypnotic dark brown eyes are filled with yearning. She takes off his glasses and runs her hand over his face. When she gets to his lips, he kisses her fingertips, then sucks on her fingers.

"Oh my God, Nathan. Nathan! Shit, I'm saying your name too much, aren't I? I'm sorry. I'm just so overwhelmed. I can't believe I'm doing this. I don't even know you."

"We're getting to know each other right now. And there's no reason to be overwhelmed. I'm right here with you. And for what it's worth..." He leans down to whisper in her ear. "I like it when you say my name."

He kisses her along her jawline until he gets to her lips, taking his time kissing them softly and slowly. He pulls out and turns her onto her stomach. Reentering her, he pumps his dick in and out, faster and faster.

"Shit, shit, shit! Nathan. Yes. More!"

"Oh, fuck. Latrice!"

~

Latrice

This is insane. This is not just the best sex Latrice has ever had, she is sure this is, hands down, the best sex anyone has ever had. He pulls out and turns her to her side, and they fuck in a spooning position while he holds her breasts and plays with her nipples.

Latrice's eyes roll into the back of her head. *Jesus Christ, this man. He's ... he's unbelievable.* He quickens his stroke as she clings to the bed gripping the sheets even tighter than before. Latrice is close. She's so, so close. Nathan pulls out again. *Oh, come on!*

"Stop pulling out!" Latrice begs.

"Sorry, baby. This is the last time. I just want to make this last and fuck you in every conceivable position I can. Turn around and face me."

She turns to face him. "Well, in that case, don't do it when I'm so close to coming."

"I promise I won't." He kisses her.

Nathan stands up. He lifts Latrice off the bed, holding her by her ass. She instinctively wraps her legs around his hips while holding onto his neck and resting her head on his shoulder. He reenters her and bounces her on his dick.

"Shit, Nathan... I... oh, God."

"Latrice! Latrice, fuck. Uhh, shit. You about to make me nut."

Both of their bodies are dripping with sweat. Latrice loses all sense of time, reality, everything but his presence.

"I'm close. I'm so fucking close."

"Come for me, Lala," Nathan orders. He squeezes her ass as he thrusts harder.

"Ahhhh!" she screams as she comes.

When he comes, he lets out a loud, aggressive curse as he clutches onto her and collapses back on the bed. His hold on her feels protective, like she's his and he would do anything to keep her. She likes it.

Nathan buries his face in her curls and inhales their fruity scent. He does the same to her neck. She giggles and squirms. He returns her smile with one of his own. Her lips connect with his, and everything ceases to exist except the two of them. The thought of never seeing him again crosses her mind, leaving her feeling sad. It must clearly be on her face.

"What's wrong, Lala?"

"Nothing. I'm fine." She corrects herself quickly and gives him a bright smile.

"You sure?"

You're by far the best sex I have ever had, and to top it off, you're handsome, sweet and sexy. But we're supposed to go our separate ways and forget about each other.

Instead, she says, "Yeah, I'm good."

Nathan doesn't look like he believes her, but he holds her tighter and stays silent. He rubs his hands up and down her back. She sinks into his arms and lets out a gentle sigh. Latrice hangs on to this moment, knowing it will soon be a mere memory.

HOT FOR TEACHER

Four

LATRICE

The next morning, Latrice is awakened to an empty room. She looks over at the side of the bed Nathan occupied and sees a note. She opens it and reads Nathan's impeccable penmanship.

My Dearest Lala,

I don't mean to sound corny but what can I say? Last night was nothing short of magical. You are an amazing woman and I truly hope that I met the expectations you (and your sister) had for your first one night stand.

Damn right he did. He exceeded them.

I'm sorry I had to leave but I had to go to work. If we never see each other again just know that I will never forget the time we spent together and I hope you find

*someone worthy of such an extraordinary mind, body
and soul. Thank you for making being stood up the best
night of my life.*
  Take Care,
  Nathan

Latrice folds the note and puts it in her purse and smiles. Nathan's right. The night they shared was magical. She gathers her belongings and gets dressed.

On the drive home, she thinks about all the stuff she has to do to get ready for the upcoming school week. It's mainly a distraction from thinking about Nathan. She tells herself over and over again it was just one-night and he's probably moved on by now, completely clueless of how difficult it will be for her to do the same.

NATHAN

Nathan sips his beer then smiles as he watches his niece, Shellie, and nephew, Tyler, play together in the playhouse his mother got them last Christmas. Labor Day is one of many days the Woodson's come together to eat BBQ, laugh and catch up on what they all have going on. At least that's how it is today for Momma, Amber and Leon. Nathan has chosen to sit around and play with the kids. Once it's been at least four hours, he's taking off. He loves spending time with his family, but he has way too much on his mind today. Latrice, job prospects, Latrice and Latrice's pussy. When his family visits hit the four-hour mark, Momma and Leon typically start reminiscing about one of Leon's many childhood mishaps, none of which include Nathan. It will be the perfect opportunity to say his goodbyes, give everyone a hug and slip out.

Nathan's mind inevitably wanders to Latrice's sweet juices, and he pivots quickly to job concerns. The last thing he needs is to be walking around aroused at a family gathering. And he can't excuse himself and go to the bathroom every time she or her pussy pop into his head. He'd be gone all day.

The morning of the best day of his life, he received a rejection email from an elementary school he interviewed for back in May. Granted, it was for a school that he wasn't that excited to teach at, but it would have been a steady paycheck. He had an interview with his dream school, Glen Oak Elementary, a few days ago. He's hoping to get hired so he'll have something to share with his mother. She worries about him a lot, and Leon is always talking about something happening with his career. It would be great for Nathan to share something about his.

Thinking about the interview leads Nathan to think about the lie he told Latrice in the note he left her. He ducked out after their incredible night together because he knew it was supposed to be a one-time thing and he didn't want to risk reverting to his nervous self and making things awkward. The truth is, he wanted more than anything to stay. Having her in his arms felt like heaven. He would have loved to spend the whole day ordering room service and fucking, but he knew what the deal was when he agreed to go to the hotel with her. So, in order to save face, he made up some bullshit about going to work when the fact is, he doesn't technically have a job.

Nathan was subbing last year, but now that it's summer, the subbing jobs have dried up. Granted, some teachers may need to take a day or two off during summer school, but the chances of that happening are slim. Summer school sessions only last four weeks. His job search is something he's downplaying to his family. If Momma knew how iffy his prospects really were, she'd force Leon to hire him. And as much as he loves his brother, he'd rather drag his balls over broken glass and squeeze lemon juice on them than work for him. Leon has always been a go-getter, which is why, when he was named as the CEO of the popular food delivery service Chomp four years ago, it was no one's surprise. He's the youngest CEO in the app's nineteen year history. Nathan's extremely proud of his brother. He's smart, charismatic and driven, but these characteristics have also made him difficult to be around. Ever since they were kids, Leon has always been abrasive with Nathan. Leon was placed with Momma when he was two, then eleven years later, Nathan was placed with them. Nathan was exactly eleven years old at the time. Leon had a whole decade of love and memories built between himself and Momma. When Nathan joined the family, things changed. Momma's focus was split between two boys, one she had since before he could form memories and the other who had trouble forming attachments. It took some time, but Nathan became close to his mother, and Leon resented it. To her credit, she worked hard to help bridge the gap between the two of them, and things aren't as tense as before. But they're still not great. All that has changed was Leon went from not wanting anything to do with Nathan to being his bully.

Leon claimed it was to toughen him up. He always saw Nathan as a pushover who was too attached to their mom, and while he didn't beat him up, he was always pressing Nathan about being stronger. That eventually turned into criticisms about Nathan's life, his decisions and his future. Which brings them to today and Leon's need to look down on his choice to be a teacher.

"Nate, watch the grill for me," Leon calls out.

Nathan drains his beer and heads over. Leon jogs back into the house, but not before giving his wife Amber a kiss. Momma Ernie fans herself and smiles at the happy couple. Amber and Leon fit the archetype of a suburban couple to a tee. He's the safe-looking Black guy who works a white-collar job, and she's the pretty blonde, white girl who never got past her Black guy phase in college. Momma approaches Nathan with a warm smile on her face. Her outfit is her usual round the house wear of a multi-colored kaftan and turban.

"Aren't they adorable?" she asks.

He smiles at his mother. "Yeah, they are."

"When are you going to bring someone home for me to meet?"

"I don't know, Momma. It's not looking too good."

"Well, what happened on your date the other night?"

"She didn't show up."

And now Latrice is back on his mind. What he wouldn't give to tell his mother about her. But that's a fool's errand. Nathan checked out Latrice's social media. She's a business owner and doing well for herself. She wouldn't want to build a life with a twenty-nine-year-old drowning in college loan debt. It's been hard not to think about how much he wants to see her again. She's not just beautiful, successful and smart. Nathan saw a vulnerability in her that made him want to protect her. He can tell the men she's dealt with before were unworthy of her. He desperately wants to show her why he is. Getting the opportunity to experience her mind-blowing pussy again would obviously be a priority, but more than that, Nathan wants to figure out more about who she is. *What made her open her shop? What are her passions? And what can I do for her to fulfill them?*

"Next time, baby. It'll happen for you. You're a catch. Don't worry, you'll meet someone soon."

Nathan looks at Leon. He's still on the phone, but Amber is now behind him with her arms wrapped around his waist. Leon brushes his fingers lightly across her hands as he speaks. Nathan lets out a sigh. His mom is partly right. Nathan has already met someone nice. Someone fantastic. Someone he can't stop thinking about, but she wouldn't want to settle down with him. Knowing he'll never see Latrice again makes his stomach churn. Last night was purely by chance. *The only way we'd see each other was if I contacted her through her shop's website and she agreed to see me. But that would be creepy.*

It's like everybody has their person but him. Ronnie lives in Michigan with his wife, Roxanne. They go around calling themselves R&R. And, of course, they're deeply in love and have two adorable kids just like Leon and Amber.

Momma's voice disrupts his thoughts.

"How is the job search going?"

"Things are looking up. My last interview went really well."

"That's good, Nathaniel. And remember, your brother is an option too. Just in case. I don't know what department he could put you in, but you're smart. So I'm sure he'd find a place for you."

Nathan gives his mother an appreciative smile. He knows her heart is in the right place. "I'll keep that in mind, Momma."

"Good."

She kisses him on the cheek and grabs a drink out of the cooler then returns to her seat. Leon comes back out and takes over.

"Thanks, man. That call lasted longer than I thought it would."

"No problem." Nathan daps his brother up.

"So how is the job search going?" Leon asks.

His tone doesn't convey loving concern like their mother's did. It sounds like what it always is, Leon's not-so-sneaky way to criticize Nathan's career choice.

"It's going well. I don't want to jinx it, but I had a follow-up interview with my top choice a few days ago, and I think I nailed it."

Nathan foolishly hopes his enthusiasm will result in Leon giving him a break on the constant job lectures. It doesn't.

"Nate, I will never understand how you can see how profitable the corporate world is and still choose to teach."

"As I have explained many times, Lee, I love teaching. And, for the record, education isn't some frivolous boon-doggle. Can you honestly say you would be where you are without your education?"

"Look, bruh, I'm not bad-mouthing teachers. I know that I wouldn't be where I am without my education. But c'mon, Nate, elementary school? Ya'll don't get paid squat. You have to buy your own supplies, and thanks to the Wild West gun laws in this country, you're all expected to be superheroes too."

"I hear what you're saying, Lee, but this is my dream. Why can't you just respect it?"

"Cause it doesn't make sense, little brother. I just don't get it. Didn't some kid throw a chair at you a few years back?"

Nathan lets out a sigh and shakes his head. *He would bring that shit up.*

Leon calls out to their mother. "Hey, Momma, remember when that kid threw a chair at Nathan?"

"Oh, lord, that was a mess. Nathaniel, I still think you should have sued the district," Momma replies.

And they're off. Leon mentions how the chair throwing incident reminds him of Lamar Tatum, a kid he went to grade school with. And now he and Momma are going down memory lane while Amber plays with the kids.

Nathan takes his seat and watches as his mother and brother joke with one another. He hears them both letting out uproarious laughter and checks the time on his phone. It hasn't been four hours yet, but he's thinking of cutting this visit even shorter.

Five

LATRICE

Latrice finishes getting ready for the school's welcome back potluck. She's ready to meet Stephanie Parker's replacement. Apparently, Ms. Parker got a better job offer at a parochial school and quit right before school started. Quincy and his classmates have had a series of substitutes during the first week. It's been like *America's Next Top Teacher*. Latrice chuckles at how everyone is treating this like a reality show instead of a serious search by the school to find the right teacher for their kids. Hell, she even found herself rooting for one of them. Quincy came home excitedly talking about how great Ms. Safi, their sub on Wednesday, was. Seeing him hyped up made Latrice hope she got the job. Some previous applicants are even being considered, and the winner will be announced tonight.

Latrice heads to the car carrying some goodies she made for the party. Her mind wanders to Nathan and what he's doing right now. Or who he's with. Maybe he's on another date. A rush of jealousy hits her. She knows she has no right to feel this way, but she can't help it. Things have gotten so bad she honestly considered buying a body pillow to pretend she's holding Nathan as she sleeps.

"Mom!" Quincy calls.

"Huh? What?" Latrice says, breaking from her trance.

"Where did you want me to put the cookies and wings?"

"Oh, right. You can put it on the floor so they don't knock over."

"Okay."

Good lord, she needs to get a grip. Quincy helps Latrice pack the car with refreshments. She carries a plastic pitcher filled with her homemade punch. She goes back for a veggie platter while Quincy carries the freshly baked chocolate chip and macadamia nut cookies and her famous lemon pepper chicken wings.

They arrive at the school in ten minutes, and she and Quincy begin to unload the food when one of the dads, Jackson Sims, rushes to them.

"Hey, Latrice. Hi, Quincy."

"Hi, Mr. Sims." Quincy smiles.

"Hey, Jackson, how was this year's Sims' family trip?"

"Wonderful. The best one yet. When Philip and I adopted Charlie and started the Labor Day trips, it was slow going, but Charlie has grown to absolutely love them."

"That's great. I'm looking forward to seeing the pics on IG."

"That's if Philip ever gets around to posting them. But enough about us, let me help you and Quincy."

"How thoughtful. Thank you." Latrice hands him the wings.

"Quincy, how has your first week back been?" Jackson asks.

"Good. I can't wait to meet our new teacher," Quincy says, his eyes wide with excitement.

Jackson leans in to Latrice and lowers his voice. "If only I could get Charlie to be that excited about school."

"Hopefully, this new teacher will be what he needs to get him hyped up," Latrice replies.

"Fingers crossed. I heard they didn't pick any of the subs, and I heard that they picked a guy."

A guy? Wow. That's a surprise. Only one of Glen Oak's teachers is a man, Mr. Lucas who teaches fifth grade.

"Really?"

"Yep. Word is Eileen—you know, Brittany's step-mom—was helping with tonight's decor when she ran into him by the auditorium. She sent out a group text, and now the single moms are buzzing about him. Apparently, he's quite a looker. They're bummed Eileen wasn't able to get a pic."

"How would she? What was she going to say to the

man? Hi, I'm Eileen. My kid goes here. Can I take a picture of you?"

Jackson and Latrice laugh.

"So this whole thing went from being a reality show to a beauty pageant," Latrice teases.

"It's still a reality show. Except it went from a teaching competition show to *The Bachelor*, that is, of course, if the guy is unattached."

Latrice chuckles and shakes her head. "Jesus."

"Exactly. It's going to be an interesting school year."

Jackson, Quincy and Latrice bring the food in and set it on the first buffet table by her place cards. She thanks Jackson and puts the place cards on each item, labeling her dishes. Quincy goes to find Eli while Latrice checks out what everyone else brought. No surprise, she and Rachel are the only ones who bothered to make anything good. This is why their food is always placed on the first buffet table every year. Rachel brought her delicious spinach and artichoke dip, sesame chicken lettuce wraps and latkes. The other moms brought things like store-bought pastries and buckets of greasy chicken. The only other mom who cooked anything was Dana. Latrice makes a mental note to stay as far away from whatever she brought. When she first made the mistake of eating Dana's cooking, she ended up on the toilet all night.

Latrice makes her way to Rachel and hugs her, Eli and Tim. The kids go back to joking around as Latrice chats with Rachel and Tim.

"Ready to meet the fresh meat?" Rachel asks.

"I'm shocked they actually hired a guy," Tim says.

"I know, right," Latrice agrees. "Jackson says that the single moms have been drooling over him."

Rachel nods. "I heard he's pretty handsome."

"Good, maybe they'll stop staring at me," Tim grumbles.

Rachel and Latrice laugh playfully at his annoyance.

"Oh, honey. You're a firefighter who looks like Thor. That's never going to happen." Rachel kisses him on the cheek, and he rolls his eyes playfully.

"Do ya'll know his name?" Latrice asks them.

"No, they're keeping it under wraps. They want him to introduce himself to everyone."

Just then, Principal Erin Tanaka takes the stage. Latrice, Rachel, Tim and the kids move closer. Principal Tanaka looks like she's about to announce who was voted prom king and queen. It's fitting, considering the decor of the auditorium. There are blue and gold— Glen Oak's school colors—streamers and balloons galore. It looks like a prom from a movie set in the 1950s.

Principal Tanaka smiles. "Hello, students and parents. Last May, we said goodbye to a legend of the hallowed halls of Glen Oak Elementary School, Ms. Cora Magrady."

Everyone applauds, and the kids cheer.

Principal Tanaka continues, "And tonight, we welcome our newest faculty member, who we hope will stay with us as long as his predecessor. Please help me welcome our new third-grade teacher, Mr. Nathan Woodson."

Say what now?! Latrice's eyes pop out of her head like a cartoon character.

Everyone applauds again, but Latrice can barely hear it. There's a ringing in her ears. The room is closing in on her, and all the air has left. Her eyes grow larger as she sees the man she fucked a week ago walk on stage. He looks sweet and delectable in his navy blue sweater that shows off those broad shoulders and wide chest, a pair of tan pants that she imagines is hugging that incredible ass of his and a pair of light brown oxfords. He looks studious with his glasses. Latrice feels light-headed as soon as he smiles. She almost forgot how entrancing his smile is.

He clears his throat, his shyness only making him more attractive. "Thank you, Principal Tanaka, and hello students and parents of Glen Oak. It's a pleasure. My name is Nathan Woodson ..."

"He's Black, Mom." Quincy looks at Latrice with a huge smile.

Her baby is so happy to have a Black man as a teacher—meanwhile, she's about to faint from shock and horniness.

"I know, buddy. That's awesome," Latrice says sounding way too exuberant. She hopes she sounded convincing and not like she's freaking out.

Quincy doesn't seem to notice his mother's behavior.

He just turns back around and listens to Nathan's speech.

Latrice tries to listen too, but all she can hear are the nasty things he said to her when they were fucking.

"Come for me, Lala."

"I want to taste every inch of your body."

"I like it when you say my name."

She snaps out of it as Nathan steps off the stage to greet some of the kids and parents.

Shit!

Latrice needs to distract Quincy and make a run for it. But before she can...

"Hi, Mr. Woodson. I'm Quincy, and I'm in your class."

Fuck me. Why did I raise this boy to be so damn polite?

"Hello, Quincy. It's a pleasure to meet you. I look forward to teaching you this year." Nathan grins.

"This is my mom."

Nathan looks at Latrice with a neutral expression. How does he look so calm when Latrice has to keep telling herself that bolting in front of her son would not be a good look?

"Hi," Latrice's voice strains to get the word out. She clears her throat and extends her hand. "I'm Latrice Richardson."

Nathan's hand closes tightly around hers, feeling strong and protective, even during a quick handshake.

"I'm very pleased to meet you, Ms. Richardson."

"Likewise." Latrice forces a smile.

She can feel sweat running down her back. The room feels like it has way more people in it than it does. Latrice needs air. Now.

Keep your shit together. You walked in on Mark's bitch ass fucking another woman. You can handle this.

"Quincy, baby?"

"Yes, Mom."

"Why don't you and Eli get some food and find us a place to sit?"

"Okay, Mom. Bye, Mr. Woodson." Quincy waves as he runs off.

"Bye, Quincy." Nathan waves back.

He turns and faces Latrice. To the naked eye, they look like a parent and teacher just chatting, but upon closer inspection, Nathan's eyes are betraying him. He sends Latrice a look that tells her if all these people weren't around, she'd be in his arms.

This is too much.

"Latrice," he breathes out.

It's barely above a whisper, but it's enough to make her look for the exit.

"Latrice, please. We need to talk."

"Nope! No, we don't. I have to... um... air." Latrice fumbles. She gives up on making a coherent sentence, letting out a frightened squeak and heads over to Rachel.

"So, I said we should do a vote on this year's school trip..." Rachel says to another mom.

Latrice slides up to her quickly with her arm looped into Rachel's.

"Sorry, I have to borrow her."

Latrice pulls Rachel away and rushes to the exit before she or the other mom can say anything.

"Are you okay?" Rachel looks at her like she's nuts.

Latrice paces back and forth. "Not really."

Latrice told Drea and Rachel about the one-night stand, but aside from the details of how amazing it was, she hadn't mentioned Nathan's name. She didn't want them to try looking for him online. It's bad enough Nadia kept trying to. Latrice didn't need to see him. She already had so many reminders of that night. Aside from his note, her mind wouldn't stop replaying what happened. Seeing his Twitter or IG would only make her miss him more. And here he is.

"What's going on?" Rachel asks.

Latrice looks at her and sees the genuine concern her friend has for her. Rachel's eyes are filled with worry.

"The one-night stand I had, his name was Nathan Woodson."

Rachel's eyes grow as big as saucers. "Holy shit! Holy shit! You're kidding. Latrice, tell me you're kidding."

"Do I look like I'm kidding?"

"What are the fucking odds?"

"I don't know, but they have to be huge, right? I mean, he's a teacher? We never discussed our jobs, and he's a fucking teacher."

"And Quincy's at that. I mean, if he ended up teaching the second or fourth graders or hell, even the other third-grade class, you could at least avoid him. But he's Quincy's teacher. I am stunned. This is insane." Rachel looks even more astonished than Latrice. "What are you going to do?"

"I..." Before Latrice can respond, the door opens behind her, and she turns and sees him. Nathan has an urgent look in his eyes until he sees Rachel, then he quickly transforms into Mr. Woodson, a friendly neighborhood schoolteacher.

"Hello, I'm Nathan Woodson." He reaches for a handshake.

"Rachel MacArthur." Rachel shakes his hand.

Latrice can tell Rachel's trying her damnedest to keep it together.

"It's nice to meet you," Nathan says, unable to hide the jitteriness in his voice.

"Yes. You too."

An awkward silence passes between the three of them for what feels like an eternity.

"You know what? I'm going to get some sex. I mean food! I... fuck me. I am so sorry, Latrice. I gotta go. Bye."

Rachel practically runs back into the auditorium. Latrice and Nathan stand even more awkwardly, looking at each other.

Finally, Nathan speaks. "I'm assuming Rachel knows."

"She does, but she's my friend. She won't tell anyone."

"Okay, who else knows besides her and Nadia?"

"My best friend Drea."

"Your business partner."

"Yeah. Wait, how did you know that?"

Nathan has an embarrassed look on his face. Like he's just told on himself.

"I, uh, kind of looked at your social media."

He did?

"You did?"

"Yeah, I couldn't stop thinking about you, and we never exchanged numbers. I considered calling your store, but I thought better of it. I didn't want to seem weird."

He's been thinking about her too. Latrice is still trying to reconcile with the fact that her one-night stand is her son's new teacher, and now he's dropped this bomb on her. Since he was up front with her, she should do the same.

"I couldn't stop thinking of you either. Nadia tried to look you up too, but she said you don't have social media. Anywhere."

"Yeah, I decided a long time ago to stay away. When you work as a teacher, anything you say can get misconstrued by a parent, next thing you know, you're out of a job."

"That makes sense."

"How are we going to do this?" he asks.

"I can't take Quincy out of school. He's been going here since he was five. He has so many friends. And I can't ask that he be placed in the other third-grade class without a compelling reason."

"And I obviously can't leave. I've been bouncing around as a substitute for months prior to the summer. I spent that time trying to find a permanent gig. I was up against some stiff competition to work here. I want to be a principal one day, and working at Glen Oak is my dream job."

Latrice sees how earnest he is about working at the school. This is clearly his passion. When she doesn't respond, Nathan continues.

"Look, I'll be professional. You don't have to worry about that. As far as we're concerned, you are a parent and I'm a teacher. It doesn't have to go beyond that. I'll just have to ignore how I feel about you."

"Okay. I'll try to do the same."

"Nice seeing you again, Ms. Richardson." Nathan reaches out to shake her hand.

Latrice shakes it, trying to ignore the warm feeling touching him gives her. "You too, Mr. Woodson."

Six

NATHAN

Nathan enters his classroom and turns on the lights. He has an hour before the kids will arrive. He takes a seat at his desk and sips his coffee. After being hired, he was given a rundown of each student by Principal Tanaka. Imagine his surprise when he saw Latrice in the crowd of parents.

This is a giant clusterfuck.

He didn't just shit where he eats, he had diarrhea.

This will not be easy. Hell, seeing her at the back to school party wasn't easy.

When she high-tailed it out of the auditorium, it took everything for him not to go after her immediately. It was clear she needed to talk to her friend. He'd given her all of five minutes before he couldn't take it anymore. Hearing her admit she feels something for him too was gut-wrenching. They have to ignore how much they want each other for at least a year. A whole year.

Nathan sent Ronnie a text after the back-to-school shindig, explaining everything. Ronnie, who is never at a loss for words replied:

RONNIE

> Goddamn, Nate. You have to be around her fine ass all year and can't do anything about it? I say you hit up the dating app again. Get her off your mind or else this year will be torture.

Nathan has no intention of using the dating app. As a matter of fact, he deleted it after his night with Latrice. He couldn't bring himself to try being with another woman after experiencing a magical night with an actual goddess.

Shit! Ronnie is right. This is going to be torture.

As if seeing her wasn't enough, he keeps getting a barrage of emails from the hotel they stayed at. Getting daily reminders of their night together hasn't helped. Nathan thinks of how luminous Latrice looked at the school gathering, in her cream-colored off-the-shoulder top and navy blue slacks. Those pants did nothing to hide that round ass of hers.

Stop thinking about that woman's ass. School's about to start.

There's a knock on the door. Nathan looks up, startled, and sees a nice-looking guy with olive skin and gray around his temples. It's Mr. Lucas, the only other male teacher at Glen Oak. They didn't get a chance to speak or meet formally at the party. Nathan didn't stay too long after the Latrice revelation.

"Hey. Sorry, didn't mean to scare you. Nathan, right? I'm Greg. How are you?"

"Nice to meet you, Greg. To be honest, I'm a little nervous. This is my first time having my own class. I've been subbing for a while."

"Don't worry; you'll be fine. And try not to be nervous. They can smell fear."

"I know. I'm trying to keep that in mind."

"Katie. Katie Spencer, she teaches second grade. She's right down the hall from you, and she has a stash of edibles she keeps in her car if you need it."

"Uh, I don't think—"

"Nathan?" Greg says.

"Huh?"

"Relax. I was just kidding."

"Oh, right." Nathan lets out a shaky laugh.

He never takes edibles when he's in the classroom, only in social situations. Typically, before a school day, he wakes up early and meditates for an hour. This morning, however, every time he closed his eyes, the same thing happened since he met Latrice. He sees her, usually naked. She was definitely naked this morning.

"You'll do great, newbie. Good luck."

"Thanks."

The chaos begins. Parents and school buses let the kids out in their respective drop-off zones. A handful of kids walk into the classroom while Nathan stands in front of his desk to greet the students and parents. Rachel comes in with her son, Eli. She sees Nathan, and any trace of the flustered woman he met a few days ago is gone.

"Hello, Mr. Woodson."

"Hello, Ms. MacArthur."

"I wanted to apologize about, you know."

"I assure you, Ms. MacArthur, that's not necessary."

"Okay, but for what it's worth, I've never seen Latrice light up that much for any guy. And I've been friends with her for years."

Nathan can't help his smile.

"I knew it. You like her too." Rachel grins.

Quincy walks in with a Black dude with a bald fade and a goatee. The man must be his father. They share similar features. Quincy is sporting a pair of white Jordans, some blue jeans and a black hoodie. All designer duds. His father is wearing a stylish dark blue business suit with a tan trench coat.

Rachel confirms his identity. "That's Quincy's dad, Mark. Latrice mentioned that he wanted to be here for the first day with Q's new teacher."

"That's nice."

Nathan watches father and son interact. Quincy walks away from his father who is talking loudly on the phone. Mark calls Quincy's name and insists on a hug. Quincy looks embarrassed, but does it anyway.

Loud horns suddenly blare into the classroom. Everyone looks confused, and some kids rush to a nearby window to find out what's happening. One of the crossing guards walks into the classroom, steaming.

"Who's the owner of the black Bentley Continental? You're blocking the drop-off zone," she snaps.

"That's my car. I wanted to walk my son into class," Mark replies.

Is this nigga for real?

The crossing guard shoots daggers at him before calming her face and addressing Rachel.

"Ms. MacArthur, where do parents park to walk in their kids?"

"The Bear Burger parking lot next door." Rachel smirks.

Nathan can see the glint in Rachel's eyes. She's definitely enjoying seeing Mark look foolish. He wonders what the story is there. Rachel and Latrice have been friends for a while, and she *clearly* doesn't like Mark.

"Sir, move your car or else it will be towed," the crossing guard commands.

"Fine. Quincy, have a good day." Mark rushes out of the room still on the phone, like he's the one being inconvenienced and not the line of parents waiting outside trying to drop off their kids. Nathan is speechless. *Aside from the assholery of blocking all those cars, he insisted on being here only to not even speak to his kid's teacher?*

Rachel gives Nathan a warm smile. "Good luck, Mr. Woodson."

"Thank you."

She leaves just as the bell rings. The kids are talking to each other, going over their respective weekends and catching up.

"Alright. Let's settle down." Nathan claps, gathering the students' attention "Now I know it's only the second week of school. You're still coming off summer break. Probably not too excited to be back at school, and I understand. When I was a kid, I hated school. A lot of my teachers weren't very nice, and I always had way too much homework."

The kids nod and make comments in agreement.

"Well," Nathan says, "I want to make this school year fun for you. I want you to learn all kinds of new and interesting things, and I want you to look forward to coming here. All I ask in return is that you try. Can you all do that for me?"

The kids give a mellow *yes* in response.

"C'mon now, ya'll can do better than that. Can you guys do that for me?" Nathan says with great enthusiasm.

"Yes!" the kids shout, mirroring him.

"That's what I'm talking about. Alright, let's get started. We're going to start with math. That will be our daily routine. Math, first recess, science, history, second recess, English, lunch then a free period to work on assignments. Any questions?"

A little blond boy raises his hand. "Are we going to get points for our homework? I heard that's what Mrs. Magrady did."

"No."

"Why not?" the blond boy asks impatiently.

Nathan looks at the place card on his desk, Brad Kopel. Principal Tanaka—very diplomatically—warned Nathan about this kid. He's basically a typical spoiled brat who is used to getting his way. He also happens to be incredibly popular. Nathan can see him becoming a disgraced senator someday.

"Because I'm not assigning homework. Unless you'd like me to, Brad." Nathan smiles.

His face turns red. He clearly wasn't expecting him to say that.

"No. No homework is good." Brad shakes his head so hard it might fall off.

"Good. I'm glad you agree. You will be graded on your assignments in class and your tests and quizzes. You will be given points for the quizzes, assignments, test scores and participation. If there aren't any other questions?"

No one else raises their hand.

"Okay. Please take out your math books."

I t's lunch break, and a few of the faculty are in the teacher's lounge. Nathan walks in and grabs his lunch out of the fridge. He's about to head back to the classroom when Mr. Lucas calls him over.

"Hey, Nathan, come sit with us."

"Okay."

Principal Tanaka walks in and makes herself a cup of coffee.

"How is everyone's day going?" she asks.

"Exhausting," Ms. Spencer says. "I swear, it's like these kids' parents give them uppers, then unleash them on us."

Greg and Erin laugh at the accuracy of her statement.

"Well, we only have a couple more hours before we return them to their parents," Principal Tanaka replies.

"Hey, Erin," Greg says, "any idea who's going to be the in the dunking tank for the carnival this year?"

"That's a good question. With Mr. Campbell retired, there's no one to fill that role," she replies.

"Mr. Campbell, the old janitor, retired last spring. He loved the carnival and would volunteer to do the dunking booth every year. It basically became a tradition," Katie explains to Nathan.

"That sounds like fun." Nathan smiles.

"Yeah, but now that he's gone, we have to find a replacement." Erin sips her coffee.

"How about Nathan?" Katie suggests.

Nathan almost chokes on his chicken salad sandwich.

"It'll be like we're welcoming the newbie with a brand new tradition," Katie explains.

"So, basically, you want to haze me?" Nathan asks.

"If it's okay with you?" Katie smiles.

"It's not hazing, Nathan." Principal Tanaka rolls her

eyes at Katie playfully. "And all the money goes to help the kids," she adds.

Nathan looks at his new co-workers and his new boss's hopeful faces.

"Alright, I'll do it," he relents.

"Yes!" Erin cheers.

As the day ends and the children meet their parents, Nathan goes over his lesson plan for the next day. He gave the kids their assignments, and for the most part, they breezed through them. He has a night of grading ahead of him so he can give them back tomorrow.

Today was good. The kids are great, funny and bright. Little Ashleigh B—there are three Ashleys in his class, each with a different spelling—is struggling with math. He wants to get her some help. She's a bright, shy little girl who needs support. Nathan wonders how much she's getting at home. Quincy is well-mannered and popular. He's smart and inquisitive. He raised his hand every chance he could to either answer a question or ask one. Nathan looks forward to getting to know him better.

This makes sense to him. This is what he does best. Working a corporate gig would kill him. Teaching allows Nathan to let go of his worries and just be. Being around kids and seeing them share themselves little by little makes it easier for him to do the same.

Without warning, Latrice walks in. Nathan takes in her enticing scent before he looks up and sees her. It's the same scent from the party and the night they met. He almost starts drooling. "Sparkle" by Cameo plays in his head. She looks like a million bucks, with her red turtleneck and a black pencil skirt that stops at her knees. The whole outfit shows off her killer figure and takes Nathan back to the hotel room. He wishes they could go back there right now.

"Hello, Ms. Richardson. Quincy went to wait for you at the drop-off zone," Nathan chokes out.

"I know. He's waiting with Rachel and Eli at Bear Burger. We're all going out for a back-to-school dinner. It's something we've done since kindergarten. We didn't get a chance to do it last week."

"That sounds like a lot of fun."

"It is. I actually came by to see how your first day went."

"It went well. Thank you for asking."

"I heard you're going to be the new dunking booth victim."

How could she possibly have known that already?

"Wow, word spreads fast around this school." He smiles.

"It does. You have big shoes to fill. Mr. Campbell was basically Mister Rogers. Everyone loved him."

"No pressure there."

"I'm sorry. I didn't mean to make you nervous."

"I'm kidding. The only thing I'm nervous about is if Ms. Spencer suggests I wear some hoochie daddy shorts and nothing else."

Latrice looks at him with hooded eyes. "If you do, I

will definitely be visiting your booth several times that night."

Nathan's dick twitches. He gets up and approaches her. "I thought we were going to play it cool, *Lala*."

"You're right. I'm sorry." Latrice bites her lip.

"Don't apologize. Just let me know which direction you want this to go in. I can be discreet." He reaches out and gently brushes her fingers with his.

The two look at each other with hunger in their eyes.

Latrice breaks first. "I should go. I'm glad your first day went well. Quincy can't stop talking about how cool you are, by the way."

"I appreciate that. He's a great kid."

"Thank you. He is. I'll be seeing you, Mr. Woodson."

"Yes, you will, Ms. Richardson," Nathan says gruffly.

Latrice walks out of the room with that sexy-ass hip sway. Nathan is suddenly a lot more excited about the dunking booth.

Seven

LATRICE

L atrice pulls up to the valet parking booth, exits her car and hands the valet her keys and fifty bucks.

"There's an extra fifty if you bring it back in this same condition," she says.

The valent grins happily, accepting the tip. "No problem, ma'am."

Latrice loves her car. Rarely does she treat herself, but to celebrate the boutique breaking its own sales record, she went car shopping last spring. She took Thad and Quincy, and they convinced her to buy her dream car, a silver Mercedes Benz E-Class.

She enters the restaurant and finds Nadia already seated. Nay Nay has already ordered their drinks. A ginger ale for herself and a sparkling water with lime for Latrice.

Latrice hugs her and gives her a peck on the cheek.

The sisters are meeting to go over plans for this year's Richardson Family Reunion happening in June. Even though it's only September, the family takes this celebration seriously. Last year, Thad was in charge and he hosted a family potluck and talent show at his place. He also paid for all the out-of-towners to stay at a nearby hotel. Everyone had a ball that weekend. Latrice and Nay Nay have no choice but to make sure their year tops Thad's.

"How about family Olympics? We can have medals made," Latrice suggests.

"As competitive as our family is? Do you remember three years ago at Aunt BeBe's house? Family game night?"

"Oh, right."

Family game night got a tad heated when Uncle Sly and Uncle Levi got into an argument over alleged cheating at Monopoly. It ended with the two men, both in their sixties, wrestling in BeBe's backyard and then the two brothers not speaking to each other for a year.

"I got it. We can rent out a whole park and have an outdoor family movie night on Friday. You know, with one of those big inflatable screens, and we can do a photoshoot on Saturday, all leading up to the barbecue at my place on Sunday," Latrice says.

"That works. We just have to figure out what movies we're going to watch," Nadia says.

"We'll do a double feature. The first movie will be something for the kids and the second for the grownups.

How about *A Goofy Movie* and *Boomerang*? By the time the grown folks movie is on, the little ones will be asleep."

"Sounds like our work is done." Nadia claps.

"Our work? I'm the one who came up with the activities." Latrice eyes her sister.

"And I agreed on them." Nadia grins.

Latrice rolls her eyes. "Whatever."

"Okay, I'll add my two cents. We should rent some food trucks, an ice cream truck and have a kettle corn vendor on hand for the movie night."

"That's my girl," Latrice perks up.

"I'm sorry, but it gets harder and harder to get enthused for our family gatherings when they cost a shit ton of money and there's still some folks who bitch anyway."

"That's true, but it is fun to see everyone. And the majority have a great time."

"Yeah, I guess."

Latrice understands Nadia's frustration. Their father, Earl, has family from Kentucky who have the nerve to expect to be wowed with each activity every year. Latrice, Thad and Nadia only participate to please their dad. The reunions used to rotate throughout the entire family until everyone decided that "Earl's kids" can plan them.

The waitress comes, and they each put in their lunch order. Latrice orders the spring salad, and Nadia orders the Ahi tuna salad.

"By the way, I still haven't been able to find your boyfriend online."

"That's because he's not on social media."

"How do you know that?"

The waitress brings them some more bread. They thank her, and Latrice butters a piece before taking a large bite while Nadia waits for her response.

"Well?" Nadia asks.

"What?" Latrice mumbles, her mouth still full of bread.

"What do you mean, what? How do you know that Nathan doesn't have social media?"

She swallows, then sips her water. "He told me."

"He told you! Bitch, you couldn't have mentioned that earlier?"

Latrice has two choices: she can pretend that Nathan told her the day they fucked and she just forgot to mention it to Nay Nay—which is not remotely believable—or she can come clean. She chooses the latter.

"Nathan told me last week."

"You saw him again? When? Did ya'll hook up? I thought you didn't exchange numbers."

"He's Quincy's new teacher." Latrice speeds through the sentence before quickly sipping more water.

"He's Quincy's what?"

Latrice clears her throat. "New. Teacher."

Nadia looks at her like she must have misheard, her eyes wide and her mouth agape. After a full thirty seconds, Nadia bursts out laughing.

"Girl, I know you lying." Nadia holds her side. "I'm so glad I wasn't drinking when you said that."

"Are you done?"

"Yes…" Nadia tries to hold in her laughter but fails. "No!"

She attracts the attention of some fellow diners.

"Hey, ya'll, this is my sister. She recently had her first one-night stand, and the guy turned out to be her son's new teacher," Nadia explains to the strangers and continues laughing.

"Nay Nay, shut the fuck up!" Latrice seethes.

"Ouch. Tough break," a man nearby says.

"Yeah, yikes," the woman with him adds.

"Both of you, hush up and eat your lunch," Latrice chastises.

"Stop tripping, Trice. I'm simply explaining so we don't get accused of being too loud and get asked to leave." Nadia looks at her innocently.

"You're the only one being too loud. You're always the only one being too loud," Latrice says through clenched teeth. "I swear to God I'm going to kick your ass."

"I'm sorry, but this is hilarious. Only something like this would happen to you. The good girl loosens up and—"

"It bites me in the ass."

"What? No, you're looking at this all wrong. Only you would have a one-night stand with a guy who has, and I quote, 'a mouthwatering dick and the most superior stroke game' you've ever experienced. And then, through some kind of kismet, stars aligning bullshit, he ends up being available to you whenever you want."

Latrice crosses her arms across her chest and listens.

Nadia continues, "Only you would have something like this fall into your lap. That's why I laughed. Even when you're being bad, it still works out for you. It's so unfair."

"Name one time that's ever happened?"

"Remember when you were sixteen and you snuck out the house for the first time and you ended up meeting Usher?"

"Yeah, and I didn't even get caught either. That was pretty fucking awesome." Latrice smiles.

"My point is, now that you have an all-access pass to Nathan's dick, you better take advantage."

"I don't know, Nay Nay."

"Don't know what? You're both adults. As long as you don't fuck on campus, what you do on your time is your business."

"He did say something the other day. I playfully flirted when we were talking about him being the dunk tank victim. He said that he could be discreet and for me to let him know how far I wanted to take things."

"There you go. He's giving you a green flag, Trice. Take it."

"What about Quincy? And what if Nathan hurts me?"

"Latrice, you're smart. You learned a lot after Mark. You'll know what to look for this time around. And I'm sure you and Nathan can work something out as far as Quincy's concerned."

The waitress brings them their salads, and they eat in silence. Latrice still isn't convinced, but she won't let Nadia know that. The split from Mark did a number on her. It's why her dating life was cut short with each relationship. She couldn't give any of those men the commitment they wanted out of fear she'd be hurt again. But even that isn't her biggest concern. How this will affect Quincy is at the forefront of her mind.

Later that night, Latrice and Quincy watch TV. She looks over at him, her little man. The most important person in her world. He looks over at her, and she smiles.

"Mom, why are you looking at me like that?"

"Because I love you."

Quincy chuckles. "You're so weird."

"Does that mean you love me back?"

"Yes, Mom." It's clear he wants to change the subject. He does that when Latrice gets too mushy.

She pauses the TV. "Hey, bud?"

"Yeah."

Latrice isn't sure how to approach this, so she rips off the band-aid and blurts it out.

"How would you feel if I started dating someone and things got serious?"

"Are you dating somebody, Mom?"

"No. I just wanted to know if my having a boyfriend would make you uncomfortable."

"Not really," Quincy starts. He thinks about his

answer. "I guess I would be okay. As long as you two didn't fight all the time like Acacia and dad."

"They still fight in front of you?"

"And the twins. I feel bad for them. At least I get to come home to you, and I have Uncle Thad and Auntie Nay Nay. The twins only really have me and Auntie Drea."

Latrice turns the TV off completely. "Quincy, I don't want you to feel obligated to spend half the holidays with your dad and Acacia because you feel like you have to protect the babies."

"If I don't, then who will?" Quincy says sadly.

Her poor baby and those poor twins. They shouldn't be raised in a household where yelling and dysfunction are the norm, and Quincy shouldn't have to shoulder the burden of protecting them. He's only eight.

"Quince. That's not your job. Your father and Acacia need to be the adults here, not you."

Latrice picks up her phone and sends Mark a text.

LATRICE

When do you have a free Sunday?

MARK

This Sunday. Why?

LATRICE

Because you, Acacia and the twins should come over for brunch. I'll cook. We need to talk.

MARK

What about?

LATRICE

You and Acacia fighting in front of Quincy and the twins.

There's a long pause before Mark replies.

MARK

Fine.

Latrice puts her phone away, looks at Quincy and smiles. "Don't worry, baby. Momma's handling this."

"Thanks, Mom."

"You're welcome, my love."

"You know, if you do get a boyfriend soon, then maybe in a few months you'll get married again and I'll have a stepdad. Eli really loves Uncle Tim. Maybe it will be the same for us."

"Maybe."

Latrice lets her imagination wander. What kind of stepdad would Nathan be like? Clearly, he likes kids, and he obviously likes Quincy. More importantly, Quincy likes him too. He came home super excited to tell Latrice about all the cool things Mr. Woodson did. She smiles at the thought. She turns the TV back on and excuses herself. After going into her bedroom, Latrice takes out her phone and calls Nadia.

"Hey, eldest sibling," Nadia answers.

"Hey, Nay Nay. I need a favor. It's about Nathan."

Nathan stands outside waiting for his students to be dropped off. After the hectic morning of his first day, he is trying something different. Starting this week, he will meet the kids in front of the school as they're dropped off by their parents or the bus. Then they'll all walk to the classroom together. Nathan knows he'll get some pushback. They are eight-year-olds after all, not babies. But he'll explain the two-minute walk from the drop-off zone to the classroom is their time to unburden themselves from the stress of the morning.

Eli gets dropped off first. It's only been a week, but he has secured his position as class clown. He's a funny, spirited child who is sometimes disruptive, but he means well. Eli and Quincy being best friends makes sense. He's the comic relief, while Quincy's the straight arrow. Those two are quite a pair. They even have their own handshake.

Eli looks just like his mom, same blue eyes and brown hair. He has freckles covering his cheeks and nose. His stepfather, Tim, looks like fucking Thor. When Nathan first saw him, he had to do a double take to make sure it wasn't really Chris Hemsworth.

"Hi, Mr. Woodson." Eli beams.

"Hello, Eli."

"Why are you outside?"

"You'll see. I'll explain once everyone gets here."

"Okay. Hey, I have a question for you."

Nathan already knows this won't be school related and will probably be a goofy joke, as Eli has brought one in almost every day since Nathan started.

"Shoot."

"What do you call a fake noodle?"

Nathan chuckles. This kid couldn't be serious if you paid him. "I don't know. What do you call a fake noodle?"

"An impasta," Eli says proudly.

Nathan laughs at the silly joke. "That's a good one."

Eli smiles. "I knew you'd like it."

Quincy gets dropped off by Latrice. She smiles at Nathan right before she drives away. It only lasted a second, but he already knows it's the best part of his day.

Quincy walks over to Eli, and they do their buddy handshake.

"Good morning, Quincy." Nathan grins.

"Good morning, Mr. Woodson." Quincy smiles back. "Eli didn't tell you his joke, did he?"

"I did, and he liked it." Eli brags.

Quincy rolls his eyes. "I begged him not to tell you."

"It's okay, Quincy. Eli's right. I did enjoy it."

"Ha! Told you so." Eli smirks.

Quincy chats with Eli as the three of them wait for the rest of the class to arrive. Once everyone is assembled, Nathan gets their attention.

"Alright listen up, ya'll. This is going to be our routine from now on. We'll meet out here and walk to the classroom as a group."

Charlie raises his hand.

"Yes, Charlie." Nathan acknowledges him.

"Why are we walking together, Mr. Woodson?"

"Yeah, we can get to the classroom by ourselves," Ashli W. says.

"I know you can. But from the time you all wake up, it's rush, rush, rush. Hurry up, get out of bed, get ready, eat your breakfast, let's get you to school. I want you all to take two minutes to get your minds right before we enter the classroom. Get your giggles out, talk, joke, whatever you need to do. Cause the minute we hear that bell, it's go time. Sound good?"

The kids nod. Nathan can tell that some are still confused or skeptical, but he knows they'll get it once they get used to it.

As they head to the classroom, Nathan sees Eli and Quincy have been joined by Ashleigh B. They're becoming a little three musketeers. Nathan wonders when the boys will teach her the secret handshake.

Nathan and the kids enter the classroom and take their seats. He begins the second part of their daily routine by asking everyone to close their eyes and breathe in through their nose and out through their mouth. They repeat the action three times.

The bell rings, and the kids open their eyes, ready to start the day. Nathan smiles as they look visibly more relaxed. He gets things going by taking roll call. Emily Chen is excused for the week due to her grandmother's funeral. Nathan's in contact with her parents through email and has been doing Zoom lessons with her after school to make sure she doesn't fall behind. He also had all the kids sign a card for her and her family, and he sent flowers.

Brad walks in late. Again. And just like the other three times, Nathan is positive he doesn't have a note. He casually takes his seat, offering no apology or explanation. This kid has been tardy four times, and Nathan's only been teaching here for a week. *What the fuck is wrong with his parents?* Nathan prides himself on being patient with his kids and their parents. But there's always one mom, dad or student who tries to get under his skin. To his credit, Nathan's been successful at not letting that happen. Not even with that little fucker who threw a chair at him. Nathan told Brad to let his mom know that if he was late again, he'd have to miss both recesses. And now comes his least favorite part of the job.

"Everyone, please take out your math books. Brad, can I speak with you, please?"

The kids take out their math books while Brad walks up to Nathan's desk looking nonplused.

"Do you remember the talk we had about your tardiness?"

"Yes," Brad replies, looking annoyed.

"Did you tell your mom about getting you here on time?"

"Yes."

"Do you at least have a note for today?"

"No. Can I go back to my seat?"

"No, and like we discussed, you're going to have to stay in the classroom during recess today. Both of them."

"Whatever." Brad scrolls through his phone.

"Put your phone away, and please look at me when I'm talking to you," Nathan orders.

The conviction in Nathan's voice makes Brad do as he's told.

"Look at your phone again, and you won't get it back until after school. Do you understand?"

"Yes."

"Good. Brad, if you're late again after today, I'll have no choice but to get Principal Tanaka involved, and detention will probably be the next step. Is that what you want?"

"No."

"Okay. I'm going to send an email to your mom letting her know what's going on. Please take your seat."

Brad sits down.

Hours later, it's fifteen minutes after three. School let out, and Nathan didn't have them all walk out together. Trying to get them to focus when they just want to go home would be like herding cats.

Dana comes in with Brad in tow, looking downright pitiful. Nathan guesses that Ms. Kopel read the email and asked Brad about it. Kids will say anything to shift blame off themselves. Parents will too. He knows they're here to tag team him. She's the put-upon mother, and he's the misunderstood kid. One would think Brad was subjected to solitary confinement instead of playing with his phone during recess.

"Can I help you, Ms. Kopel?" Nathan asks.

"Yes. Look, I know you're new here, but there's a way things are done at Glen Oak. Brad has been attending this school since kindergarten, and he's an exceptional child. There are times when he may run late due to our daily rituals."

"Daily rituals?"

The routine Nathan has implemented is for the kids' benefit. He doesn't see how being late for school could benefit Brad.

"Yes. I read Brenda Daniels-Quintero's book, and she said the best way to help gifted youngsters thrive is to allow them to have at least thirty minutes of alone time. It just so happens that Brad does his between seven and seven thirty every morning, depending on how he's feeling."

Nathan doesn't even know how to respond to that. It's clearly written all over his face because Dana continues.

"His last teacher understood. Can we expect the same from you?"

"No."

"I'm sorry?"

"Ms. Kopel, I am not going to give Brad a pass to be late every once in a while because a reality star said it's okay."

"Brad is gifted, Mr. Woodson."

"So are a lot of the kids in this school. That doesn't give them carte blanche to do whatever they want."

"Brad, go wait in the car."

"Yes, Mom." Brad sends a pitiful look her way.

"It's okay, sweetie." Dana kisses Brad on the top of his head.

Nathan resist the urge to roll his eyes.

Brad leaves, and Ms. Kopel gets close to Nathan. *Real* close.

"Maybe we could come to some other arrangement...?" she says, her voice husky.

Dana's fingers graze the top of Nathan's hand. She attempts to take his hand in hers.

What the fuck!

"Oh, no! No, no, no, no, no. No, Ms. Kopel."

Nathan backs away, separating them by standing behind his desk.

"Alright, here's what's going to happen. I'm going

to pretend you didn't do that, and you're going to start bringing Brad to school on time," Nathan instructs her.

"Come now, Mr. Woodson. I saw the way you were looking at me last week."

"What?"

Nathan realizes what she's talking about. Last week, Dana—on one of the few days she actually brought Brad to school on time—came in with Brad right as Latrice was dropping off Quincy. It was the second and last time Latrice ventured into the classroom. Just as she was getting ready to say something to him, she got a text and had to leave. Nathan snuck what he thought was a discreet look as she walked out. She was wearing tight jeans that day.

Aw, shit!

Nathan tries to think of something quick before Ms. Kopel pulls out her titties or something.

"Ms. Kopel, there has been a gross misunderstanding. I'm seeing someone, and I had just gotten off the phone with her when you walked in. That's why I looked so—"

"Horny."

"I was going to say 'enamored.'"

"So there's no chance you and I...?"

Hell motherfucking no!

Nathan simply says, "No. I'm sorry."

"Oh well, it's your loss."

Dana leaves, and Nathan releases his breath. He's

gotten hit on by mothers before, but it's never been that predatory. He takes a seat at his desk.

Jesus Christ.

Nathan opens the door to his apartment. He lays his attaché case on the coffee table and grabs a beer from the fridge. After undoing his tie, he lies on the couch. His phone buzzes. It's a number he doesn't recognize. He puts his phone back in his pocket, and it buzzes again. Nathan sighs and retrieves it, seeing he has two text messages. He's about to toss his phone on the table when something tells him to read the messages.

LATRICE

Hi Nathan.

It's Latrice. I got your number from Nadia and have been working up the nerve to contact you. Don't ask how Nay Nay got it. Just know that she has her ways. I wanted to send you a quick text so you can save my number in your phone. Give me a call sometime.

Nathan stares at his phone for a minute without blinking. He takes his glasses off, cleans them then puts them back on to make sure he hadn't misread the words on the screen.

He leaps from the couch and pumps his fist in the air.

"Yes!" he shouts.

He calms himself down. What should he say when he texts her back? He takes a seat and starts typing.

NATHAN

Hi Lala. Does this mean you'd like to continue what we started at the hotel?

Nathan reads over it, not wanting to come across as desperate. He hits send and says a quick prayer. His phone buzzes.

LATRICE

Maybe. I'm seriously thinking about it.

NATHAN

Please let me know when you've come to a decision.

LATRICE

Nathan you should know by now, I have no problem letting you know when I'm coming.

Dear God, he wants to marry this woman.

LATRICE

I'm looking forward to seeing you in those hoochie daddy shorts at the carnival. I heard it will be a warm seventy five that day.

NATHAN

I'll be there butt naked if you want me to.

LATRICE

LMAO! Not necessary but thank you. Don't want you getting all the other moms riled up.

Nathan briefly thinks about his encounter with Dana. He cringes at the memory.

NATHAN

Definitely don't want to do that.

LATRICE

I'll let you go. Nice chatting with you, Nathan.

NATHAN

You too, Lala.

He places his phone on the coffee table and gets up to fix himself dinner. He takes out the leftovers from dinner at Momma Ernie's and reheats them, his mind racing. Nathan has a renewed purpose. Now that he knows Latrice wants more than just "parent" and "teacher," he needs to figure out how to turn her maybe into a yes.

Nine

NATHAN

Over the next couple of days, Nathan and Latrice talk on the phone every night into the wee hours of the morning. She waits until Quincy is asleep and calls him around nine at night. By that point, he has graded every assignment so he can devote all his attention to her. They've avoided anything too heavy, instead talking about where they went to college—UC Davis for him, UCLA for her—where in the world they want to travel and even if this entire world is just a simulation.

Tonight's topic is music.

"What song do you consider your guilty pleasure?" Nathan asks.

He's walking around his apartment in a white T-shirt and black sweatpants with bare feet, wondering what Latrice is wearing. Every time he wants to ask, he chickens out. Even though he feels at ease with her, he still gets jitters talking to her like he's the quiet, bookish kid trying to ask out the head cheerleader.

"Promise you won't make fun of me?"

"I would never make fun of you."

"I don't know if I believe that," Latrice jokes.

"Okay, how about this? If I did make fun of you, you would be in on the joke."

"Alright, I'll buy that. Before I tell you, please know that I will defend my choice."

"Understood."

"'Open Your Heart' by Madonna."

"That's not embarrassing. That's a catchy song. Honestly, the whole *True Blue* album is pretty good."

"I know right!"

"I mean, there is a reason why she's part of the trinity."

"The trinity?"

"Yes, in the 1980s, the holy trinity of music was MJ, Prince and her. Now having said that..."

"Here we go. I knew you were going to roast my choice."

"Nope, not roasting. I'm just clarifying that despite Madonna's place in the trinity, Janet is the queen of pop."

"Oh, hell yeah! And not because Mike is her brother."

"Not at all. She earned her title just as much as he earned his."

"Agreed. So what's your guilty pleasure song?"

"What do you think it is?"

"I don't know. 'Baby Got Back'?"

"That song isn't a guilty pleasure, Lala. It's an anthem for brothas."

Latrice laughs, and Nathan can't help himself.

"Your laughter makes my heart soar," he admits. When she doesn't say anything, his face heats up. "I'm sorry. That was corny."

"No, it wasn't. Hearing me laugh really makes your heart soar?"

"Yes, it does."

"Wow. That's probably the best compliment I have ever been given."

"I can top that."

"I don't know, Nathan. That was pretty good."

"Hop on FaceTime. I want to see your face when I say this to you."

Latrice video calls him. He answers, and his breath is taken away from how gorgeous she is. She's one of those beauties that does not need a stitch of makeup, but when she wears it, she looks so ethereal. Her face is currently free of any cosmetics and looks fresh and clean. She has a headwrap on and smiles when she sees him.

"Nathan?"

"Yes."

"Why is it every time you see me, you look at me like it's the first time?"

"Because that's how it feels."

"Thank you. So what was the better compliment than your heart soaring?"

Nathan looks deep into her eyes. "You make me want to be a better man."

Latrice looks touched, but soon, her flattery turns into tears.

Shit!

"Lala, I'm sorry. I didn't mean to make you uncomfortable," Nathan pleads.

Why did I say that? Now she's going to get spooked. Maybe talking every night wasn't a good idea. They were bound to get into more personal stuff, and Latrice obviously isn't ready. It's evident she has some concerns about what's happening between them. Coming on too strong isn't helping.

She calms down and wipes her eyes. "No. Don't be sorry. Nathan, no man has made me feel as special as you do."

How is that fucking possible?

Now he is just confused. "You're telling me that no man that you have been with has ever told you how brilliant, captivating and sexy you are?"

"Not in so many words. I mean, I've gotten compliments from men, but they never sounded as impassioned as you."

"Then they were all fools. Especially your ex-husband."

"What do you know about Mark?"

"Not much, just that he's an idiot for letting you get

away and an entitled dipshit who parked his car in the drop-off zone."

"Yeah, Quincy told me about that. And you're right. He is super entitled."

"May I ask you a question?"

"Sure."

"What happened between the two of you?"

"That's a long story."

"I'm not going anywhere."

Latrice gives him an appreciative smile.

"Markus and I met in 2014. He swept me off my feet, and I fell for him hard and fast. We got married three months later. Everyone thought it was too soon, but I was in love. Nine months to the day we got married, Quincy was born. It didn't take long for Mark to start getting distant. Whenever I wanted to talk about it, he'd dismiss my concerns. The cheating started shortly after. I foolishly forgave him after he promised not to cheat anymore, and things were good for a while. At the time, I was a stay-at-home mom while Mark worked as a financial manager for Enerex, a renewable energy company. He's now the CFO."

Nathan takes a seat on the couch and listens. He nods his head, encouraging her to continue.

"When Quincy began going to daycare, I decided to go back to work against Mark's wishes. With a loan from my parents, I started Mtindo. After the boutique's first year, we were already turning a profit. Then I recruited my friend Drea—Mark's sister—to work alongside me.

That pissed Mark off. He thought I was choosing Drea's expertise over his."

"So he's an entitled idiot who's painfully insecure." Nathan states it plainly.

"Yep. Leaving him was the best decision I ever made. At one point, Mark tried to get me to close the store."

"What?"

"You heard me. He said that he made more than enough money, so I didn't need to work."

"Wow. We both have narrow-minded asshats in our families."

"Who's yours?"

"My brother."

"Your turn after I'm done."

"Okay."

Nathan isn't sure about telling Latrice about his upbringing. He's not embarrassed about being a foster kid, and he loves his family. He just gets uneasy when talking about his past and his relationship with Leon. But he's going to do it. For Latrice, he finds himself willing to do anything.

"Anyway, when trying to make me quit didn't work, he tried to tell me how to run it. When it became evident that his help wasn't needed, Mark got distant again. One day, I came home to find Mark in bed with Acacia—his current wife. He tried to talk me out of the divorce, but that was the last straw. I packed up my shit and left. I didn't try to take him to the cleaners. I even let him keep the house. I just wanted my son, and to be rid of that man. And that's what I got."

"Good for you. You put yours and Quincy's well-being first."

"I had to. I'm not going to lie. What happened did some damage to my ability to trust. The men after Mark all wanted something more, but I wasn't ready."

"And what about now?"

"Honestly, Nathan, I don't know. I have Quincy to think about, and with you, it's more complicated given your relationship to him."

Hearing this disappoints Nathan, but he can't blame her. He blames her ex. If he could, he'd punch that worthless motherfucker the next time he sees him.

"I understand. I'm not going to push you into anything you're not ready for, Lala."

"Thank you. I appreciate that. Okay, now it's your turn. I want to hear the story of Nathan Woodson."

He lets out a chuckle.

"Alright, well, first things first. As you know, I'm the youngest of two boys, but honestly, I could have more siblings I don't know about. I'm a foster kid."

"Wow. Do you know anything about your biological parents?"

"Not much."

"Who named you?"

"My first foster mother."

"Your first?"

"Yeah, first of fifteen."

"Wow, I know I said that already, but…"

Nathan gets up to prepare himself a cup of tea. He turns on the stove and adds water to a kettle.

"It's okay. Fifteen foster homes from birth to age eleven is a lot. Momma got me when I was eleven and adopted me a year later. That's how I got the last name Woodson. It was Blanchard before. Literally, the only thing I know about my biological mother."

"Fifteen different families in eleven years."

"Yes, ma'am."

He picks chamomile. Talking about his upbringing is inevitably going to cause some anxiety, and he'll need something soothing to get through it. He contemplates adding Henny as he reminds himself to pick up some more edibles.

"Did any of your foster parents… I mean, were you ever…?"

He can hear the reluctance in Latrice's voice. He knows what she's trying to ask.

"Abused?" he finishes the question for her.

"Yeah." She sounds almost embarrassed for asking.

He goes ahead and adds a splash of Henny to his mug.

"Unfortunately. I was six, and she beat and insulted me pretty regularly. She felt my being quiet and reserved was a sign of disrespect. I'm pretty awkward socially, as you may have noticed."

"Honestly, Nathan, I just see it as shyness. I'm not

trying to downplay anything you've gone through, but you always seem comfortable around me."

"That's because I am. Don't get me wrong. My attraction to you does cause me to be nervous in your presence sometimes, but for the most part, I enjoy it. I enjoy how you make my stomach knot up with anticipation when I wait for the kids to arrive every morning. You're very overwhelming in the best way."

"Thank you."

"You're welcome."

"I'm sorry, continue."

"It's alright. Anyway, my guardian was hurting me for something I couldn't help. The years from birth to age eleven are huge for social development, but I bounced around so much that by the time I was six, I didn't know how to interact with people. When she would introduce me to anyone, I wouldn't speak. She thought I was being rude. Thankfully, that was the only home where that happened, and I was removed after five months."

"I'm so sorry, Nathan."

"Thank you."

"Can I ask you another question?"

"Of course."

"Is there anyone else in your life that you're this comfortable with?"

"Yes. Momma, my boy Ronnie and my students. I'm obviously not this candid with the kids, but I do let my guard down with them. I find it's easier with them. Besides, they can smell bullshit a mile away."

"That they can. You don't have any other friends besides Ronnie?"

"Not really. I had associates that I've met from subbing, but after a while, you lose touch."

"When did you meet Ronnie?"

"In high school. That's how long it took me to let my guard down and start trying to make friends. Momma took me to a therapist when I was thirteen, a Black dude too. Talking to him made me feel like conversing with people wouldn't actually kill me."

Latrice chuckles. "I'm sorry. I shouldn't laugh."

"No, it's okay. I can make jokes about it now. Even at twenty-nine, I still have my moments of *'shit, I have to talk to people now, don't I?'* but it's not nearly as bad as it once was."

"Is that what you were thinking when you got up and gave that speech at the welcome back shindig?" Latrice teases.

"Jesus Christ. When Principal Tanaka offered me the job, I was over the moon. I actually did a happy dance."

"You, sir, will have to show me that dance sometime."

"Bet."

They both laugh.

"I was so happy, Lala. After months of looking for work, I got hired at my first choice school. Then she dropped the bomb about me giving a speech, and it was like a record scratch."

Latrice laughs even harder.

"You're going to wake up, Quincy," Nathan playfully chastises.

"Please, that boy sleeps like the dead. We're good. By the way, I enjoyed your speech. I mean, I liked what little I heard. I was pretty shocked when you came out on stage, so I didn't hear all of it."

"Yeah, the deer in the headlights look you had on your face was kind of a giveaway."

"Shut up! Like you weren't shocked too."

"Oh, I was hella shocked. I kept thinking, 'make your way over to her, and hash this out,' but then you ran."

"I was freaked out. Leave me alone."

Nathan laughs so hard his eyes are watering.

"But seriously, I'm glad you're at Glen Oak."

"Me too."

They stare at each other like two emojis with heart eyes.

"I think you should try asking one of your co-workers to hang out with you."

"Even though talking is easier, approaching and meeting new people isn't. That's why I was using a dating app. By talking to women on the app first, it gave me time to get comfortable with the idea of meeting them in person."

"You didn't have trouble checking me out the night we met."

"Yeah, but if you recall, Nadia called me over. I didn't approach you. And I have a confession. When you and I were exchanging looks, I was literally telling myself, 'okay, smile, but not too much. Look at her for a few seconds, then look away. Don't stare.'"

"You obviously did a great job of talking yourself through it."

"I've had a lot of practice."

"Is that how it's been with you typically? Women always approaching you?"

"Yeah. Every girlfriend or fling has spoken to me first. Ronnie likes to joke that I make women work for it, but I honestly still struggle with walking up to anyone and starting a conversation."

"Give it a try with one of the other teachers. Ask one of them to go out for beers or something."

"Like an adult playdate?"

"Exactly."

"I guess I can give that a try."

"Good. Now, tell me why your brother is a narrow-minded asshat."

He takes a sip of his tea. *Ugh!* He forgot he added the henny.

What the fuck was I thinking?

"Oh, my God!" He chokes.

"Are you okay?"

"Ugh, shit." He pours the tea down the drain.

"Nathan?"

"Yeah, I'm here. Jesus Christ, that was disgusting."

"What was?"

"I made myself some tea, and I added some liquor to it. We're talking about deep, personal shit, and I thought I could use some liquid courage. That was such a bad idea."

"What did you add?"

"Henny."

"Eww. That stuff taste like ass. Why would you drink that?"

"It's gross with tea. By itself, it's not bad."

He rinses his mouth out and gargles.

Latrice burst out laughing. "Go brush your teeth."

Nathan does just that before grabbing his phone and returning to the living room. "Much better. Where were we?"

"Your brother."

"Right. Don't get me wrong, I love Leon, and I know that, in his misguided way, he also loves me. But when I arrived, he was thirteen and had been with Momma since he was two. I was not just a new addition to the family. I was a kid who needed extra attention."

"Of course. Given everything you went through, it makes sense that your mother would focus on you a bit more to make you feel welcomed and loved."

"And that's exactly what she did. Leon wasn't thrilled about it and began to fuck with me. He wouldn't beat me up or anything, but he would say things like giving me warnings not to mess up or Momma would get rid of me. I was already thinking that I wouldn't be there long.

His needling just made it worse. Momma figured out what he was doing and sat us both down. She made it abundantly clear that we were both her sons and I wasn't going anywhere. Leon started acting nicer, but I could still feel his resentment. As we got older, he started to belittle my life choices. He still does. And to be honest, I don't think he does it out of concern. I think he does it to make himself feel better about his own choices. He followed the corporate path, makes a ton of money, married a beautiful woman he adores and has two great kids, but somehow still needs to pick on me."

"Why is he so pressed about what you're doing?"

"I think it's because, despite all his success, he's still a thirteen-year-old boy who has to compete with a brother he didn't ask for."

"That's ridiculous. He's a grown-ass man."

"I know, but some things are difficult to move away from. No one gets that better than me. That's why I try to stay cool whenever he goes on one of his tears about me being a teacher. He's constantly reminding me how broke and stressed I am."

"That's so fucking childish," Latrice says, sounding protective.

Nathan can't help it. He smiles at how possessive she sounds.

He looks at his phone. *Holy shit! It's three in the morning.*

"I hate to cut this short, but look at the time," Nathan tells her.

"Oh, my God! We need to stop talking this long."

"You keep saying that, and yet."

Latrice smiles. "I know. I know. Goodnight, Nathan."

"Goodnight, Lala."

"Oh, wait!" Latrice pipes up just as Nathan is about to end the call.

"What's up?"

"You never told me what your guilty pleasure song is."

"It's not a regular song; it's from a musical."

"I'm intrigued. Tell me."

"'Helpless' from *Hamilton*."

"I love that song!" Latrice beams.

"Me too."

I also think I'm starting to love you.

Ten

LATRICE

atrice, Thad, Nadia and Drea take Quincy from one ride and attraction to the next. Nadia came to the carnival to make trouble for Latrice and Nathan, Drea came to prevent it and Thad came because he knew Drea was coming.

The line for the dunk tank is insane. Latrice sees Nathan, and while he's not wearing hoochie daddy shorts, he is wearing basketball shorts and a white T-shirt. Nadia gets in line. It's a dollar per try. Nadia gives three dollars. So far, no one has gotten Nathan wet.

"What are you doing?" Latrice asks.

"I'm about to get your boyfriend all wet and give you a show." Nadia smirks.

"Nay Nay!"

"What? Bitch, you're the one who asked for his number, which you probably haven't used yet."

"As a matter-of-fact, I did, *bitch*."

"Really?" Nadia looks over at Nathan. His eyes are fixed on Latrice.

"Guessing by the way he's looking at you, your little chat went well."

"Chats. We've been talking regularly since I first texted him."

"Are you going to resume your tryst?"

"I'm thinking about it."

"Thinking about it? Girl, stop thinking, and let that man dick you down."

"How were we raised by the same people?"

"Your guess is as good as mine. I used to think I was adopted."

"If I hadn't been in the room when mom pushed you out, I would have thought so too."

Thad and Drea approach. Thad has a corn dog while Drea has a large plush panda bear.

"Where did you get that?" Latrice asks.

"Thad won it for me." Drea grins.

"Really?" Nadia teases.

"Yeah, I hit the bell while playing on the high striker," Thad says casually.

"He got it on the first swing," Drea brags.

"That's right! These arms aren't just for show." Thad winks at Drea.

She giggles as she cops a feel on one of Thad's biceps while Latrice and Nadia share a look. Thad and Drea's situation makes as much sense as a soup sandwich. They flirt, give each other goo-goo eyes and they each can't stop talking about one another when they aren't around each other. But they won't take it any further. Seeing them so obviously into each other but refusing to pull the trigger makes Latrice think about how she's doing the same thing with Nathan.

"Stop overthinking," Nadia says.

"What?" Latrice snaps out of it.

"You are doing that thing with your face when you're thinking really hard," Thad replies.

"Whatever. Did ya'll see where the Family MacArthur went with Quincy?" Latrice asks.

"They're in line for the Tilt-A-Whirl," Drea replies.

"Well, between winning stuffed bears and getting corn dogs, you two have been taking your sweet time getting back to us," Latrice complains.

"Didn't realize we needed to chaperone you the whole day," Thad teases.

"You know damn well it's our sister that needs to be reined in. Drea, I thought you were going to make sure Nadia didn't start any shit," Latrice says.

"Oh, you mean with Q's teacher?" Thad grins.

Latrice's eyes grow large. She looks at Drea like she's going to kill her.

"Don't look at me. You know damn well your loud mouth sister can't keep a secret," Drea defends.

Latrice turns and looks at Nadia angrily. "Goddamit, Nay Nay!"

"What?" Nadia says.

Latrice gets up close to Nadia so they're almost nose to nose.

"Why did you go and tell T about Nathan?" Latrice demands.

"I needed a male perspective and, for the record, everyone agrees with me, even Drea."

Latrice turns to her friend. "Seriously?"

"I mean, I still think you should tread lightly considering who he is to Q, but Trice, I have never seen you this lit up. You should have seen the look on your face when you described your night with him. I will still make sure Nay Nay behaves—I mean, as much as I can—but I think you should at least get to know him and see where it leads," Drea argues.

"And I have to hand it to you, Trice. I didn't think your goody-two-shoe self had it in you to do some shit like that," Thad adds.

Latrice looks at her siblings and her best friend. They all smile at her, giving her the support she needs to try and figure out what she should do. She looks at Nathan, and his eyes catch hers. She smiles and waves. He smiles and waves back.

Maybe they're all right, Latrice thinks.

Latrice and Nathan are gazing intensely at each other when he suddenly falls into the dunk tank. Latrice looks at Nadia, who is laughing her ass off and doing a victory dance.

"Yeah, that's right!" Nadia yells.

Latrice frowns at Nadia, who looks back and mouths "what?" to her.

Nathan rises out of the water and climbs out of the tank. The whole thing looks like it's happening in slow motion, like when Phoebe Cates climbed out of the pool in *Fast Times at Ridgemont High*. Latrice swears she can hear the same music accompanying Nathan as he lifts his shirt and takes it off. His muscles glisten with the droplets of water running down his body. The basketball shorts cling to his strong thighs. Latrice can't look away. And, apparently, neither can the other moms. Dana's looking at Nathan like he's a six-course meal. Noting everyone's reaction, he rings his shirt out and quickly puts it back on. It's pointless though. The shirt is now transparent, and the outline of his insanely ripped body is as clear as day.

He turns his attention to Nadia and smirks. "You got lucky."

"Whateva, negro." Nadia grins.

Nathan looks over at Latrice who is still in a trance when Quincy runs up to her excited and hugs her. Rachel, Tim and Eli are with him.

"Mom, you have to get on the Tilt-A-Whirl. It was so much fun!"

Latrice laughs. "Maybe later, Quince."

"Mr. Woodson, come here. I want to tell you my new joke!" Eli bellows.

"Eli, Mr. Woodson is in the middle of something," Rachel says.

Nathan jogs over. "Okay, Eli, but you have to make it quick."

"How do all the oceans say hello to each other?"

"I don't know. How?" Nathan smiles.

"E, do you know every joke in that book?" Quincy asks.

"Yep. This is never going to end," Eli says in a playfully menacing voice.

Nathan bursts out laughing as Latrice watches his interaction with the kids, and it's clear how much they mean to him. Aside from observing Nathan's blatant sexiness, Latrice noticed how patient and kind he was whenever a kid tried to dunk him. When they missed, he'd encourage them to try again.

"They wave!" Eli says. "Get it?"

"I get it. I think that's my favorite one so far."

"By the way, Mr. Woodson, you look like a superhero." Eli grins.

Nathan smiles. "Aquaman?"

"No, I mean, you look like you could be one. You should dress as one for Halloween."

"Yeah, you could be Black Panther," Quincy says with great enthusiasm.

"Tim's going to be Thor," Eli says.

"That's fitting." Nathan smiles at Tim.

"Yeah, well, the little guy makes me dress up as Thor every year, so." Tim shrugs.

Quincy pipes up. "Mr. Woodson, this is my Uncle

Thad, my Auntie Drea. And my Auntie Nay Nay is in line to dunk you."

"Nice to meet you." Nathan shakes Thad and Drea's hands. "And your Auntie Nay Nay has already dunked me, so we're well-acquainted."

"Don't feel too bad. Nay Nay used to play softball. You were going to end up in that tank no matter what." Thad pats Nathan on the back.

"I don't know if I should feel less embarrassed or more." Nathan laughs.

"Hey, Mr. Woodson. Get over here. I still have two more tries!" Nadia calls out.

"Duty calls." Nathan chuckles. "See you all later."

Nathan jogs back over to the tank and reclaims his spot. The line is now even longer with all the moms who were ogling him getting back in line.

"Mom, can we please get food? I'm starving," Quincy asks.

"Sure, sweetie."

Everyone but Nadia heads over to where the carnival food is. She joins them a few minutes later, after dunking Nathan two more times.

When they're done eating, visiting the petting zoo, riding the Tilt-A-Whirl—which almost made Latrice puke—the carousel, bumper cars and the Ferris wheel, everyone is ready to call it a day. Nadia, Thad and Drea say their goodbyes and take off.

Latrice leans over to talk to Rachel. "I'll be right back. I'm going to use the ladies' room before we leave."

Rachel smirks. "Tell Nathan goodbye for me."

Latrice giggles. "Will do."

She heads over to the dunk tank but doesn't see Nathan. Her heart sinks.

"Looking for me?"

Nathan's sexy voice gets her attention. She turns around and sees that he's changed into a pair of light gray sweatpants and a matching hoodie with a dry white T-shirt underneath.

"Hi." Latrice smiles.

"Hi." Nathan grins back.

"We're getting ready to head out, and I didn't want to leave without saying goodbye."

"That's very thoughtful of you."

"How much did the dunk tank make?"

"The carnival total was fifteen thousand, with five hundred coming from the dunk tank."

Latrice nods her head and tries to hold in her laughter. "Nice. Mr. Campbell used to drum up at least a hundred annually during his tenure. So I'm guessing this means you're going to be doing this every year now?"

"Yeah. Principal Tanaka has pretty much made it a decree."

They laugh. Latrice's smile lingers as she and Nathan study each other.

"Did you at least get a break? Did you eat?" she asks.

"I had a hot dog in between dunks."

"That's all you ate? I feel like I should make you something now."

"I mean, if you want to feed a brother, I won't say no."

"Okay. But I can't tonight. I can make you something tomorrow. Come by the shop to pick it up. I have an appointment with a client at three. Stop by before then."

"Thank you. Does one o'clock work for you?"

"That's perfect. You got any food allergies or dietary restrictions?"

"None."

"Good to hear. I'll text you the address."

"No need. I googled it after we met, remember?"

"Of course. I'll see you tomorrow Nathan."

"Looking forward to it, Lala."

Latrice walks away, making sure to add a little more sway to her hips since she knows he's watching. She turns to check and, sure enough, there he is. His eyes are glued to her ass. When he looks up at her face, she smiles and winks. He lets out a low groan that tells her she'll be making an appearance in his dreams tonight.

Eleven

NATHAN

Nathan finishes his final set of crunches. He woke up at 2 a.m. unable to sleep, and masturbating isn't helping as much as he'd like. Every time he closed his eyes he saw Latrice. This caused him to hop out of bed and head to the gym. After a quick warm-up on the treadmill, he went hard on the weights, working his upper body, then used the machines for his lower body. Finished with his core workout, he lies on the floor, catching his breath. The exhaustion weighs on him. He closes his eyes and sees Latrice's face. Her dimples, that wink she gave him, the extra wiggle in her hips as she walked away. When he goes to her boutique, it will be for more than just her cooking. He's going to get that "yes" he's been craving.

The next few hours are a tortuous slog for him. At a quarter after twelve, he grabs his keys and wallet and heads for the door when his phone buzzes. It's his mom.

"Hello, Nathaniel."

"Hi, Momma."

"Are you busy?"

"I'm actually getting ready to leave."

"Oh, well, I was hoping you could help me with something. It shouldn't take too long."

Nathan knows his plans for the day have now officially changed the minute his mother said, 'It shouldn't take too long.' Because, with Ernestine Woodson, it always takes too long. The last time she called him to help her with something that "wouldn't take too long," it took him six hours. She needed a ride to run her errands because her car was out of commission, but she failed to tell him that one of those errands included visiting her friend Gertrude MacAfee. Ms. MacAfee's an incredibly sweet woman who insists on feeding folks the minute they walk through her doorstep. Nathan ended up taking home a week's worth of leftovers. He is incredibly disappointed that he won't be getting laid, but he tries to comfort himself with the idea of getting fed.

"What do you need help with?"

"It's the water at the house. I don't know what's going on. I mentioned it when I spoke to Leon, and he said he would send someone over. I waited all day, but they never showed up."

Nathan wishes she had just called him. Momma and Leon may be close , but he's not the one she should go to when she needs help. Sure, his career pays better, but it doesn't leave him with a lot of time to spare. Nathan once called Leon to catch up and after they spoke for five minutes, Leon had to put him on hold. After thirty minutes, Nathan hung up. The next time they saw each other, Leon admitted he forgot Nathan was on the other line. Nathan wouldn't be surprised if Leon just plain forgot to call somebody for their mom.

"I'll be right over, Momma."

Nathan sends a text to Latrice letting her know he can't come by the boutique today. Typing the words sends a sharp pain to his chest. He missed out on a night's sleep thinking about this woman, and now he can't even see her. He shakes it off. Momma needs him. He'll make it up to Latrice later. She sends him a response, telling him it's okay and that she'll just have to feed him some other time. He thanks her for understanding, silently hoping she's not too upset.

Twenty minutes later, he arrives at Momma's. He opens the door to find her in sweatpants with her hair tied up in a ponytail watching "The First 48" while snapping green beans.

"Hi, Momma." Nathan kisses her on the cheek.

"Hi, baby."

"What exactly is wrong with your water?"

"It's brown."

"I'm sorry, what?"

Momma Ernie looks up at Nathan. "All the water is brown."

"How long has your water been brown?"

"A couple of days."

"Your water's been brown for days and you're just now telling me?"

"I immediately called you after I didn't hear from Leon or whoever he was supposed to send by here."

"Momma, you should have called me first. Promise you'll call me first from now on."

"You fuss too much."

"Momma," Nathan urges.

"Okay, Nathaniel. I will call you first."

"Thank you. How have you been cooking or taking showers?"

"Ms. Rojas next door has been letting me use her shower, and I've been using bottled water for everything else."

Nathan sighs. "I'm going to check out your water heater."

"Thank you, Nathaniel."

Nathan takes a look, and everything seems normal. It has to be her pipes. One of his previous foster fathers was a plumber who occasionally took Nathan with him on jobs. Momma has put Nathan to work many times to fix things over the years. She has lived in this house for thirty years, and while Leon has paid for many upgrades, there are still more that are desperately needed.

He heads for the door. "I'm heading over to the hardware store, Momma. I'll be right back."

"Oh, Nathan, while you're out, could you get me some stuff from the store?"

"Sure. What do you need?"

"Not much, just juice, peaches, brown sugar, flour, a tray of chicken legs—"

"Momma?"

"Yeah, baby?"

"Text me a list of what you need."

"Okay, sweetheart. Thank you!" She smiles.

Nathan comes back two hours later. It takes him another four hours to install a water filtration system. By the time he's done, he's exhausted and ready to go home. Momma Ernie insist that he stay for dinner, which takes another hour. When he finally leaves her house, it's eight o'clock at night.

Desperate to salvage his day, Nathan drives by Latrice's shop on the off chance she's still there. He praises God when he sees her car in the parking lot. He'd recognize that silver Benz anywhere. She has a specialty license plate: LtriceR.

~

LATRICE

Latrice is in her office sending an email to an up-and-coming designer who just won first prize on *The Wow Factor*. It's the most popular fashion reality show since *Project Runway*. Latrice is addicted to it. The premise is unique and fun. An aspiring designer is teamed up with an aspiring fashion model. The designer has to come up with runway ready looks each week surrounding a specific theme using the model as their muse. Each episode ends with a photoshoot and an elimination from the judges. The winning model gets a contract with a top agency, and the winning designer gets a job at the House of Helena, working under none other than Helena Dupar, the grand dame of all fashionistas and a dear friend of Mtindo.

Latrice rarely works this late, but it's a Saturday and Quincy's spending the night at her parents' house and is no doubt being spoiled. He always has a ball when he goes there, and with the brunch from hell rescheduled for tomorrow, Latrice thought it would be nice to give Quincy a nice respite before a family confrontation. Mark canceled it at least four times before finally agreeing to the new date.

Latrice's mom wasn't too pleased to hear that she invited Mark and Acacia to her home, but Latrice thinks it's important that Quincy be in a comforting environment during the discussion. He deserves to be heard too. After all, the twins aren't the only ones being affected by Mark and Acacia's behavior.

Latrice stretches and lets out a yawn. She locks up the filing cabinet and walks out of her office. She hears the sound of a sewing machine and knows it's Ingrid, hard at work making something incredible. Latrice stands in the doorway of the back storage room and sees Ingrid doing some finishing touches on a dress she designed. When Latrice saw how talented her designs were, she had some sewing equipment put into the room especially for Ingrid. She uses it to work on her class assignments.

"Ingrid, go home," Latrice orders her employee playfully.

"I should say the same thing to you." Ingrid smiles.

When there's a knock on the boutique door, they both look at each other, confused. No one ever comes to the shop this late. Ingrid puts away the dress she was working on and follows Latrice as she heads to her office. They look at the live feed from Latrice's computer to see who it is.

It's Nathan! He sent a text message earlier saying that he wouldn't be able to make it. Latrice was disappointed, and it didn't help that he didn't go into any real detail about why. He just said a family issue came up. As much as she hates to admit it, it brought back memories of when Mark was distant with her and came up with excuses for why they couldn't spend time together.

She presses the button on the intercom. "Hello, Nathan."

He presses the intercom button and replies, "Hi, Latrice. I came by on the off chance you were still here. I wanted to apologize."

"It's fine."

He chuckles. "No, it's not. I apologize for canceling on you last minute. I swear if it was something I could have avoided or rescheduled, I would have."

"What happened?"

"My mother had brown water, and I had to fix her plumbing."

Latrice certainly wasn't expecting him to say that. "Is everything okay?"

"Yeah, it's all good now."

"I'm heading home. I still have your container of wings if you still want them."

"Yes, of course."

Latrice gathers her things.

"Latrice, not to overstep, but who is that gorgeous man?"

"A friend."

"Does he have any brothers?"

"He has one, but he's married."

"Ugh, boo!"

Latrice laughs at Ingrid as she enters the code to the security system and locks up the shop. She and Ingrid walk out together. Ingrid smiles and waves at Nathan. He politely waves back.

"Nathan Woodson, this is Mtindo's store associate, Ingrid Miller."

"Nice to meet you," Ingrid says.

"You too," Nathan replies.

He clearly didn't think anyone else would be here. His awkwardness is evident. He takes a look at Latrice and pivots quickly, turning to address Ingrid.

"How long have you worked at Mtindo, Ingrid?"

"Almost three years. I love working here. I'm learning

so much, and it's great to have a Black woman as a mentor."

"Are you aiming to own a clothing boutique too?"

"No, I want my own clothing line. I want my brand to be as big as Versace."

Nathan gives her a nod, looking impressed. "Okay. So, in other words, I will never be able to afford your clothes. Good to know," he jokes.

Ingrid laughs. "Don't worry, you'll get the friends of Latrice discount."

"Why, thank you. I appreciate it."

"Well, I'm going to get going. It was nice to meet you, Nathan."

"You too, Ingrid."

Ingrid gets in her car and drives off, waving at them. Nathan and Latrice wave back before facing each other.

Nathan looks at her like she's a prize he just won. The look of desire is palpable, but it's the admiration she sees in him that makes her heart race.

"Why are you staring at me like that, Mr. Woodson?"

A smile emerges on his handsome face. He looks damn good in an unzipped black hoodie, a maroon shirt, blue jeans and white sneakers. His long legs fit those jeans perfectly. She is tempted to ask him to turn around so she can check out his ass.

"You're amazing," he replies.

"How so?" Latrice smiles.

"You built this shop and made it into something so incredible that every A-lister shops here. And now you're helping to make Black women more visible in fashion. You. Are. Amazing."

Latrice's face flushes. "I just gave a part-time job to a hard-working, talented young woman. All the success Ingrid will have will be because of how amazing *she* is."

"Don't do that," Nathan commands softly.

"Don't do what?" Latrice asks.

"Don't downplay how big of a role you're playing in Ingrid's future. She knows how lucky she is to be working alongside you. It's going to open so many doors for her. I'm sure every single designer who works with Latrice Richardson knows that trusting her with their work will only yield greatness for them. Don't downplay all that you have accomplished, Lala. "

Latrice feels the tears forming in her eyes. "Thank you."

Oh my God, I'm falling for this man.

Wait, what?

Yes, no other man had ever made me feel this way, but that's no reason to start tripping.

They stand there staring at each other for a moment before she hands him the wings.

"Here."

"Thank you."

He opens the container and inhales the amazing aroma. Even though they've been in Latrice's mini fridge all day, they can still smell the seasoning.

"These smell amazing."

"Thank you. They're chipotle lime."

"I can't wait to try them. Thank you."

"You're welcome."

"Well, I don't want to keep you. I just wanted to apologize face-to-face."

"I appreciate it."

Nathan heads to his car.

Don't just let him leave. Stop being so goddamn scared.

"Nathan?" Latrice calls out.

Nathan stops and turns to face her. "Yes?"

"Do you want to come home with me?"

Twelve
NATHAN

Nathan assumes he must have imagined Latrice inviting him to her home, so he asks her to repeat her question.

"Do you want to come home with me?" she asks again.

"I would love to come home with you, but what about Quincy?"

"He's staying at his grandparents' house. He's not due back until tomorrow around ten. As long as you're gone by the time he comes home, we'll be fine."

"And your neighbors? I'm assuming most of them are Glen Oak parents as well."

"They are, but it's dark enough that no one will be out, and you can park down the street from me. There's a large parking lot near the Trader Joe's. People park there all the time, and no one ever gets a ticket. You'll be fine.

Just throw your hood on before you make your way to my house."

"You've thought of everything."

"I've imagined this scenario numerous times."

"Lead the way."

Minutes later, Nathan makes himself comfortable on Latrice's couch. Her home is beautiful. It's a one-story, single-family house that holds so much character. The modern design and internal decor match her well.

"Your house is stunning."

Latrice hands him a glass of wine. "Thank you. Would you like a tour?"

"Yeah, I'd love that."

She tells him she used her divorce settlement to buy the house. It was built in 1950 but remodeled the year before she purchased it. It has an open floor plan and a light-filled entryway with vaulted ceilings. There are hardwood floors throughout. Her chef's kitchen has quartz countertops and Bertazzoni stainless steel appliances. There's an entertainment space and three bedrooms, including her primary suite with a large walk-in closet. She shows him the spacious backyard with beautiful landscaping and stylish outdoor furniture before they make their way back to the living room. Latrice kicks off her shoes and takes a sip of wine.

Nathan finishes his, then places the glass on a coaster on the coffee table.

"Look at you with the manners." Latrice places her glass next to his.

"I was raised right."

They share a laugh.

He looks around, still in awe of her home. "I'm scared to ask how much this cost?"

"Almost two million," Latrice says casually.

Two million dollars! Nathan can't fathom having two million dollars at all, let alone two million dollars just to buy a house. The idea of Latrice seeing his apartment fills him with anxiety. What would she think? She knows he doesn't make as much money as her, and she isn't a judgmental person. Still, the idea of her seeing his shoebox of a home makes him flush with embarrassment.

"Are you okay?" she asks.

"I'm fine."

She doesn't look like she believes him, so he takes her feet and lays them in his lap. Nathan immediately gets to rubbing, hoping to distract her. Latrice lets out a moan that makes him shift on the couch. Latrice moves her foot so she's rubbing Nathan's erection. He puts her feet down and climbs on top of her, forcing her to lie on her back. Their faces are inches apart. Nathan can't take his eyes off her. She's a dream come true. He rubs his nose against hers and she giggles.

"I need you, Lala."

"You do?"

"Yes."

"You need me to do what?" she teases.

He grins. "I. Need. You. You need me too. I saw it. I saw it in the way you looked at me during the carnival."

"And how was I looking at you?" Latrice asks softly.

"The way you're looking at me now." Nathan kisses her over and over. "I need you," he whispers.

He makes his way down her face, peppering her with kisses.

Nathan stands up and lifts Latrice from the couch, carrying her to the bedroom. He lays her on the bed gently, backs away and takes off his clothes. Latrice places a hand on her chest, looking at him like he's a prize. Nathan smirks. He loves the effect he has on her.

"What would you like me to do to you first?" he asks.

"You decide."

Nathan shakes his head and strokes his dick. "Nope. That's not what I asked you, sweetheart."

Latrice takes deep breaths. Nathan picks her up and holds her in his arms.

"I have never felt this way about any woman before. I have never wanted to let someone in as much as I do with you. All I want is to be near you all the time. You're like a drug, Latrice. A wondrous drug that gives me a high that I cannot come down from."

He sets her down and gets on his knees, looking up at Latrice with conviction in his eyes. His hands slide up her skirt as he takes off her panties. He removes her skirt, blouse and bra, then climbs back onto the bed. Taking her hand, he kisses it.

"Now what would you like me to do first?"

"Kiss me."

He kisses her. Taking his face in her hands, she kisses

him back with vigor. Their kiss is carnal and demanding. Both of them communicate through touch how much they ache for each other. He palms her ass and squeezes. Her full breasts are pressed against his chest, and his heart beats with increasing intensity. He feels hers beating just as hard. They refuse to detach from each other. Their tongues meld, unable to separate. Their hands explore every inch of each other's body. Nathan's dick is as hard as granite. She breaks their kiss and catches her breath.

"Do whatever you want to me, Nathan," Latrice pleads.

Without saying a word, Nathan flips her over and lays Latrice on her stomach. He runs his tongue over the crack of her ass and bites her left cheek.

"Mmmmm," Latrice whimpers.

Nathan takes a gentle bite of the inside of Latrice's ass.

"Oh, my God. Shit." Latrice pants.

Nathan spreads her butt cheeks and runs his tongue up and down the inside of her ass. He tickles her asshole with his tongue.

"Oh, fuck. Nathan!" she squeals.

Latrice turns over and stares at him, dumbfounded.

"That feel good?" He chuckles.

"Yes, but, my God."

"You getting wet?"

"You know I am. Why would you even ask that?"

He lets out a jubilant laugh before spreading her legs open and licking her wet pussy. When Latrice squirms,

Nathan lightly tickles her clit with his tongue, causing her to giggle. Wrapping his mouth around her folds, he takes in her juices like a lifesaving elixir.

"Oh, shit. Shit!" Latrice cries out. Wetness slides down to her ass. Nathan licks it right up, then sucks on her clit.

"Nathan," Latrice begs. "More. Please. More."

"Are you sure, Lala?"

"Yes, please."

He responds by planting gentle kisses all over Latrice's pussy and inner thighs.

Nathan gets a condom from his pants pocket and rolls it on before crawling back on top of her and sliding his rock-hard dick inside of her.

"Fuck," Nathan stutters.

They lie like that for a minute, with her arms around his neck and him holding her thighs while his dick throbs inside of her. Her pussy tightens around him just like the first time. Latrice moves her hands to his face. Staring at each other, he moves, thrusting deeper. Latrice raises her hips to match him.

"Damnit, Lala. I—oh, God."

Nathan squeezes her breasts together and sucks on her nipples. It's too good. He never wants this to stop. Latrice crosses her legs, trapping him as he pushes himself harder and faster. She lifts Nathan's face and kisses him.

"You like tasting your pussy on my lips, Lala?" Nathan asks.

"Yes. It makes me want you more," she whines.

She deepens their kiss, sucking on Nathan's bottom lip and giving it a bite. He forces his tongue back into her mouth. Latrice releases a series of indecipherable moans as she comes. Only one word is clear.

"Nathan."

"Latrice. Oh, fuck."

Nathan pulls out, yanks the condom off and comes on her stomach. He gets up and goes into her bathroom. Coming back with a moist towel, he wipes her off, then lies back down next to her. She touches him, tracing her fingers along his chest and stomach slowly.

"I don't know what's happening between us, Nathan, but I know I want more of it."

"I can't speak to what's happening to you, Lala, but I'm falling for you. I'd like to see where this goes," he admits.

LATRICE

Latrice takes him in. This incredible man. Her hands are still on his body. He shivers as she gently touches his wide, strong back. Her hands make their way to his ass.

"We have to be careful," Latrice says.

"And we will. Look how careful we were tonight."

She is so relaxed. Her eyelids are heavy. All that

matters in this moment is her and Nathan. He holds her close as she runs her fingers all over his body. He leans over, his lips lightly caressing her ear.

"I'm glad I was able to turn your 'maybe' into a 'yes.'"

"Me too."

While taken aback by Nathan's declaration, Latrice is excited to explore this next step with him. Even if she's more than a little scared.

"I want to see where this goes, but I haven't been in a serious relationship since Mark. It's not easy for me to trust another man with my heart. And what about your job? And Quincy?"

"Don't overthink it, Lala. We'll take our time and figure this out together."

With those words, her body melts into his. He massages her scalp, and her eyes close in slumber.

It's two in the morning and Latrice is awakened to find Nathan gone. She looks to see if he left a note like at the hotel. When she doesn't see one, she instantly regrets telling him he had to be gone before morning. Falling asleep in his protective hold was divine. She thinks about what he told her as she snuggles deeper into the blankets, inhaling his scent. Just as she's about to drift back to sleep, she hears a noise in the kitchen. *Shit!* She reaches down and retrieves the baseball bat from under her bed. After putting on a robe, she creeps into the kitchen only to find–

"Nathan?" She looks around in confusion.

Nathan turns to her and appears alarmed.

"I got hungry. I didn't think you'd mind. But I can put the Doritos back. They aren't worth getting beat down over."

Latrice places the bat on the coffee table and walks over to him. She wraps her arms around his waist and rests her head on his chest. He lets out a deep chuckle and kisses her on top of the head.

"You scared me." She giggles.

"I'm sorry, sweetheart. I didn't want to wake you."

Nathan eats some Doritos and pulls something out of the pantry.

"Oh, snap! Fruit snacks. I have to say, hooking up with a single mom is the smartest thing I have ever done. Y'all have the best stuff."

Latrice laughs. "Are you going to eat up all my son's snacks?"

"Of course not. But don't trip. Quincy and I are cool. He won't mind sharing."

They both laugh.

"I sometimes forget how young you are," Latrice says, snatching a Dorito from his hand.

"I'm not that young," Nathan complains.

"I am much older than you, sir."

"*Pfft*. You're thirty-eight. That's not that much older."

"Oh, wait."

Latrice retrieves the wings from her refrigerator and heats them up.

"That's right. We were so busy, we forgot about those." Nathan walks up behind her and bends down to kiss her neck.

"Mmmm," Latrice moans.

The more he kisses her, the more addicted she gets. She takes the wings out and hands him one.

"Wow," he says after taking a bite.

"Good, right?"

"This is amazing."

"We each have our specialty for family dinners. I handle the wings, Thad has smoked meat or barbecue on lock and Nadia does oxtails."

"I'm going to have to try all of that," Nathan says as he takes another wing.

Latrice smiles, but her face turns pensive quickly.

"Nathan?"

"Yes, Lala."

"I know my concerns about us, but do you have any? Like, does it bother you even a little that I make more money than you?"

Nathan seems to think it over. "I'll admit. I was a little intimidated by how nice your house is and how well off you are. It made me think that my little rinky-dink apartment wouldn't be good enough for someone as classy as you."

"I wouldn't care about that."

"Logically, I know that, but it is a thought that has been running through my mind. But to answer your question, no. I am not at all bothered by what you've accomplished."

"I know you're impressed, but—"

"There is no 'but,' Latrice, and I'm not just impressed. I'm proud of you. I really am."

"Thank you."

"Besides, I've always wanted a sugar momma." He smirks.

She bursts out laughing and hits him playfully. He laughs and grabs her arms, pulling her to him. Lifting her up, he holds Latrice by her thighs and carries her back to the bedroom before stopping.

"What's wrong?" Latrice asks.

Nathan turns around, grabs the wings and bag of Doritos then jogs back into the room with Latrice laughing.

"**M**om!" Quincy calls from the living room. Latrice's head shoots up and she looks at her phone. It's ten in the morning. *We overslept.* And Nathan is still asleep.

Fuck, fuck, fuck!

"Trice, baby. We're here with Quincy," her mother calls out.

Double fuck!

Latrice shakes Nathan awake.

"Wha? What's going on?" Nathan says in a daze.

"*Shhh!* Quincy's home. And my parents are here," Latrice whispers.

"What? It's only..." Nathan checks his phone. "Oh, shit! I'm so sorry, Lala. I must have slept through my alarm," he admits in a hushed tone.

"Don't blame yourself. I did too."

"Mom?" Quincy calls again.

"I'll be right out, sweetie," Latrice calls out.

Latrice turns to Nathan, panicked. "You got to get the fuck out of here!"

She throws his clothes at him.

He catches his pants. Latrice opens her bedroom window and pulls Nathan to it, ready to push him out.

"Lala, I'm still naked!"

"Hurry up and put your clothes on, then hide in the closet. I'll stall them."

"How do I get out of here without anyone seeing me?"

Latrice paces around the room, snapping her fingers and trying to think. She reaches for her phone and sends a hurried text to Rachel, who lives a few houses down.

LATRICE

Let Nathan stay over and we overslept. Quincy and my parents are now home. Do me a favor? Let me know when the coast is clear to sneak Nathan out.

RACHEL

I got it! Manning the window now. And don't think for a second we aren't going to talk about your little sleepover later.

LATRICE

Yeah, yeah. I know. Thanks!

"Okay. I got Rachel checking for when the coast is clear. When she lets me know we're good, I'll text you. You hop out the window, then it's the same as last night, throw on your hoodie and go to your car. Got it?"

"Got it." Nathan nods.

Latrice heads for the door when Nathan takes her arm and pulls her to him. He crashes his lips against hers. She backs away, her heart aflutter. She smiles and sighs. He winks at her.

She throws on a T-shirt and shorts before running out of the room. When Latrice enters the living room, she gives Quincy a quick kiss, then hugs each of her parents.

"Baby, go ahead and get your Gran Gran and Pop Pop something to drink."

"Okay." Quincy grabs a bottle of juice from the fridge and pours a cup for everyone.

Once he's settled, Latrice sips her juice but tastes nothing. She's doing her level best to not to trip over her son's teacher hiding in her bedroom closet.

"How was your visit?" Latrice asks, trying to keep her voice even.

"It was great, as always. You know how much we love seeing our grandbaby." Her mother, Janet smiles at Quincy.

For the next twenty minutes, Quincy and her parents take turns telling her about all the fun they had.

Before Latrice can respond, the toilet in her ensuite

bathroom flushes. Everyone pauses and looks at her with confusion.

"Latrice is someone here?" her mother asks.

Seriously, Nathan?! Why the fuck did you do that?

"Huh?" Latrice sputters.

"I asked, is someone here?" her mother repeats.

Think of something. Think of something!

"No, my toilet has been doing that all night. Just randomly flushing." Latrice rushes through her explanation.

"It's probably just the flapper. I'll go take a look." Her father, Earl gets up.

"No!" Latrice quickly blocks her father from going into her room.

With the way things are going, Nathan might sneeze or something. She needs to get her parents out of here and distract Quincy.

"That's not necessary, daddy. I've got a plumber coming any minute now."

"No need to pay for something I can easily fix, sweetheart," Her father argues.

"Daddy, please. It's okay. You and mom should go enjoy the rest of your Sunday. I know you two have a farmer's market to hit up. I've got it taken care of."

"Alright, baby." Her father hugs her, followed by her mother.

"You let me know how the brunch goes," Her mother says softly in Latrice's ear.

"I will, Mom."

After walking her parents to their car and waving to them as they drive away, Latrice tells Quincy to pop by Rachel's to visit Eli.

"I'll let you know when your dad is here."

"Okay." Quincy heads over to Rachel's.

Unfortunately, there are still some people walking their dogs out and chatting with neighbors.

Whatever ya'll are talking about can't be that damn important. Take your asses inside.

Latrice waves at a couple of neighbors before going back toward her room. Heading straight to her closet.

"Nice going, Mr. Woodson." She looks at Nathan with playful annoyance.

"I am so sorry, Lala. What did you tell them?"

"I told them the toilet had been flushing on its own all night. My dad almost came in here to fix it!"

Nathan rubs the back of his neck in embarrassment. "Shit. I am so sorry."

Latrice shakes her head as her phone buzzes. She takes it out and reads Rachel's message.

RACHEL

The boys are in Eli's room, and the street is all clear.

LATRICE

Thanks.

"We got the go ahead. You can head out. Text me when you get home."

"Will do."

They kiss one last time before Nathan throws on his hood and climbs out of her window. She lets out a deep breath. Next up, the brunch from hell. She's going to need a stiff drink before the day is over.

Fourteen

LATRICE

Hours later, Latrice hears Mark's car as he pulls into her driveway while she takes the quiche out of the oven. As grateful as she is for last night's distraction with Nathan, it was still a close call. He sent her a text assuring her that no one saw him and he got home okay. They both agreed to be more careful in the future. But thanks to him, she isn't nearly as anxious as she would be about this talk with Mark and Acacia.

The doorbell rings.

"Quincy, can you please answer the door?"

"Okay, Mom."

He gets up from the couch and lets Mark, Acacia and the twins in. The twins both hug Quincy. Seeing this makes Latrice smile. Quincy is such a good big brother, and those babies are crazy about him.

Mark hugs Quincy, followed by Acacia who

promptly takes a seat on the couch, not even addressing Latrice.

This is going to be fun.

Mark enters the kitchen and gives Latrice an awkward hug. She hugs him back as a show of solidarity for the kids' sake. Mark has nothing on Nathan. Yes, Mark is fine, but that and financial security are really all he has to offer. Meanwhile, Nathan's willing to offer her all of himself. Thinking about it can't help but make her smile.

"The food will be ready in another ten minutes."

"Auntie Tricey, can we go outside and play?" Leticia asks.

"Sure, baby."

All three kids go outside. Latrice turns her attention to Mark and Acacia, who are sitting on opposite sides of the couch looking at their phones.

Yep, this is going to be a hoot.

Minutes later, everyone takes a seat at the table. Latrice helps the little ones into their new booster seats she picked up a few days ago while Quincy sits next to his dad. She serves everyone and takes a pitcher of orange juice and places it on the table. Acacia is still staring at her phone.

Latrice sits on the other side of Acacia. "Well, go ahead, everyone. Dig in."

Everyone else eats their food while Acacia picks at hers.

After thirty minutes of eating and awkwardness, the

kids are back outside playing. As much as Latrice wanted Quincy to be part of the discussion, the tension is just too thick so she decides to send him and the twins to the backyard. The adults are still at the table.

"I think we should go ahead and discuss the elephant in the room," Latrice starts.

"What do you mean?" Acacia asks in an acerbic tone.

"What I mean is, you and Mark constantly fighting in front of the kids."

"Latrice, what happens between me and my husband really isn't any of your business."

"The hell it's not. You're arguing in front of my child and making him feel like he has to protect Jelani and Leticia."

"Protect them from what?" Acacia snaps.

"From the two of you. These two babies only ever see you two fighting, which makes them rely on Quincy for any normalcy."

"So? What's the big deal? He's their big brother," Acacia says.

"Do you want to jump in here?" Latrice asks Mark.

Mark sighs, then clears his throat. "Latrice, Quincy is a good kid. When he sees something is wrong with the twins, he steps in. Why should we stop that?"

Well, it's clear why these two are together. They're both insane.

"He's eight! Our eight-year-old son shouldn't be the only adult in the room."

"Fine. We won't fight anymore. Happy?" Acacia rolls her eyes.

"I'd be a lot more happy if you actually took this issue seriously," Latrice says.

Mark pours himself a glass of juice and cuts himself another piece of quiche and takes a bite.

"This quiche is amazing, Latrice," Mark says.

"Thank you but that isn't the point." Latrice replies flatly.

This makes Acacia roll her eyes. "Typical." She scoffs.

"Don't start," Mark warns her.

"You're the one starting shit, Mark. I should have never agreed to come here. This is just going to give you another excuse to belittle me. 'Latrice is better at this, Latrice is better at that. She can cook, she has a career and she's an amazing mother.'" Tears form in Acacia's eyes. She turns her attention to Latrice. "You're perfect, and no matter what, I will never measure up to you. "

Mark scoffs. "You don't even try. All you do is spend my money."

"Maybe you should have thought about that before you started fucking me!" Acacia yells.

Before Latrice can get a handle on what's going on and what to do, Acacia gets up and rushes out of the door. Seconds later, her Audi can be heard burning rubber out of the driveway. It's then that Latrice realizes that Acacia and Mark didn't even drive to the house together.

"What was that?"

Quincy pipes up. "That's what they do every time I go over to their house." He says sadly.

Latrice turns and sees all the babies. Jelani is covering his ears and crying while Leticia looks down at the floor with her head resting on Quincy.

Good lord. Latrice knew Mark was an asshole, but this is a whole new level of assholery. She and Acacia may not like each other, but there is no need for Mark to further pit them against each other. This explains why Acacia is always pretty hostile toward Latrice. If your husband is constantly comparing you to his ex-wife, there's bound to be some resentment.

Latrice gets up and gathers the children in her arms, comforting them.

"Can we stay here, Auntie Tricey?" Jelani asks.

"Yeah, can we stay with you?" Leticia looks up at her with sad eyes.

How can I say no?

Latrice will just have to work from home tomorrow. The twins are four, so it's not like they'll be missing school.

"If it's okay with your daddy, then yes."

Mark wipes his hands on a napkin, then sips his juice. "It's fine."

"I don't want to spend holiday break with you and Acacia," Quincy says without warning.

"At all?" Mark asks.

"Nope. I want to go to Gran Gran and Pop Pop's with mom."

"I get it. Why would you want to be around two screaming adults and get stuck babysitting the whole time? Look, Quincy, how about you and I do something after Christmas break? Just the two of us."

"It's okay, Dad. You don't have to make promises you won't keep."

Latrice can actually see Mark's heart breaking. After what he just pulled, he deserves to be reminded of how much of a disappointment he is to his son.

"I'll hire someone to stay with the twins, and I'll send Acacia to a spa or something. Then you and I can go wherever you want."

The desperation is painful to watch. Mark loves Quincy. Latrice knows this. He loves all his kids, but he's a selfish piece of shit and has been his whole life, making it impossible for him to be a good parent. Quincy can clearly see his father's desperation too.

"Okay, Dad. That sounds good."

Mark smiles. He stays for another couple of hours, promising to talk to Acacia.

Latrice washes dishes while Quincy and the twins play in Quincy's room. Mark will come by to pick up the twins tomorrow night.

Latrice can't help but feel like this whole plan was a complete bust. Nothing was accomplished. Acacia stormed off, Mark made empty promises again and, worst of all, Quincy and the twins heard more arguing. Latrice isn't sure what to do. She doesn't want her son to have no relationship with his father, but Mark needs to step up. Acacia too. Yes, Mark treats her like shit, but hell, she could leave him, making life easier for her and her children.

Quincy comes out and grabs some juice boxes for himself and the twins.

"That was really sweet of you to agree to spend time with your dad, Quince. And who knows, maybe you guys will get to do something this time." Latrice kisses her son on the forehead.

"Mom?"

"Yes, sweetie?"

"Could you ask Uncle Thad if he's free the weekend I'm supposed to hang out with Dad? You know, just in case."

"Sure, bud. No problem."

"Thanks." Quincy heads back to his room.

Yep. This was a complete fucking bust.

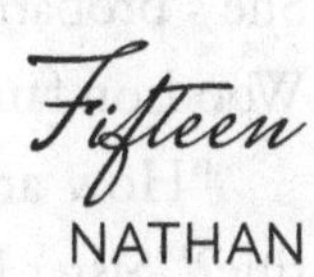

NATHAN

Nathan helps Momma out of the car and takes her arm in his. She's part of a neighborhood walking group. This morning, she and her fellow walkers did their usual neighborhood stroll, but Momma pulled a muscle. Nathan had to hop back in the car after arriving at his apartment and showering. He wasn't even dry when Momma Ernie called, asking him to come early and help wrap her foot. They barely made it to the noon mass.

Nathan has never been religious, but he attends church every Sunday with Momma. She insists they come a little early so she can chat with her fellow parishioners before the service begins.

"It's okay, Nathan. I can walk on my own."

"Are you sure?"

"Yes, baby. I'm fine."

Nathan lets her go as they enter the church. Sister

Mary Beth approaches. Momma Ernie is one of the few Black parishioners at St. Anne's. Being a Catholic church in Los Angeles, the congregation is mostly Hispanic and Latino. Most of the folks who come here love Ernestine and have frequently invited her to their family gatherings. She's probably been to more quinceañeras this year than Woodson family barbecues.

"How are you doing this fine morning, Ms. Ernestine?" Sister Mary Beth beams.

"I'm doing just fine, sister." Momma Ernie smiles.

"Nathan, we heard the good news about your new job. Congratulations."

"Thank you, sister."

"Yes, we're all happy for Nathan. I couldn't be prouder of my baby."

Nathan blushes. No matter how old he gets, he'll always love hearing his mother brag about him.

"We are so proud of you too. Helping young ones build a path to bright futures is not an easy task. I'm sure their parents are grateful to have a fine young man such as yourself enriching their lives. It's highly admirable work you're doing, son," Sister Mary Beth says.

"Again, thank you. I'm just trying to keep up with everything you've been doing here, sister. Your work with neurodivergent kids here at the church should be commended."

"Why, thank you, Nathan." Sister Mary Beth smiles. "You two take your seats. We'll talk after the service."

Nathan and Ernestine nod in agreement. They take their seats in a nearby pew.

"What was that?" she asks, impressed.

"What do you mean, Momma?"

"All that talking you were doing with Sister Mary Beth? You're usually polite, but you're never that talkative."

"I don't know. I just felt like telling her."

Nathan thinks about Latrice and how being with her has inspired him to be more verbose and try to connect with people more. She's been a miracle to him.

"Nathan?" Momma Ernie interrupts his thoughts.

"Yes, Momma?"

"You're smiling, son. What's gotten you so happy all of a sudden?"

Nathan's happy to finally tell his mother, though he wants to tread lightly since this thing with Latrice is still new.

"A woman I met."

"Really?" Momma Ernie grins. "Tell me about her. What's her name?"

"Latrice."

"That's a pretty name. What's she like?"

"Gorgeous, smart. Sometimes I can't even believe she's real."

"How did you meet her?"

"At a restaurant. I met her when I got stood up on that date a while back."

"And why am I just now hearing about her? That date was over a month ago."

"We're taking things slow. I didn't want to say anything too soon."

"I guess I understand that. Well, I can't wait to meet her. She must be something special. I've never seen you this lit up before."

"She truly is."

The church service starts, and Nathan zones out. He thinks about Latrice. It's only been a couple of hours since he left her house, and he can't wait to see her again.

~

LATRICE

Latrice wakes Quincy and the twins and helps them to his room. With brunch turning into a complete shit show, Latrice decided to treat the kids to a fun day. She took them to Quincy's favorite Chinese place for lunch, followed by ice cream and a marathon of Marvel movies at home. She tucks them in and kisses them each on the cheek. Her phone buzzes. It's her mom.

"Hi, Mom."

"How did the talk go?"

"About as well as you would think."

Her mother lets out a sigh. "Trice, baby, that man is not going to change, and his wife... ugh, don't even get me started on her. Mark seriously downgraded when he married her."

"Mom, don't. I found out that Mark's been chastising Acacia, comparing her to me. It's just a big mess all around."

"Well, that's unfortunate. I'm sure she's regretting hooking up with him now. The damage Mark is doing to Quincy, those babies and now her, is horrific."

"That's true. I don't know what to do."

"Baby, just be there for Quincy and for the twins as much as you can."

"That's what I'm doing. The twins spent the rest of the day with me and Quincy. They're sleeping in his room now."

"That's good. At least Jelani and Leticia will grow up knowing there is an adult who has their backs. On to other news, tell me about this new guy."

Unbelievable! Does my whole family know? Should I be expecting a call from Aunt Millie in Florida too?

"I'm going to kill your daughter." Latrice sighs.

"Why? Nay Nay didn't tell me. Thad did."

"Damn momma's boy."

"Language, Latrice."

"Sorry, Mom. What did Thad tell you?"

"That he's younger, and Nay Nay is the reason you met."

Whew! Good, so she doesn't know he's Quincy's teacher. Latrice can just imagine how her mom would react.

"Is there anything you would like to tell me about him?"

"His name is Nathan, and he works in education."

"Anything else?"

"Um..."

"Like the fact that he's Quincy's teacher."

Fuck! Latrice is going to kill Thad.

"Um..."

"Latrice Tamika Richardson."

Aw, Shit. She broke out with my whole government name.

"Yes, ma'am?"

"What on earth are you thinking?"

That I'm a grown adult and can sleep with whoever I want, Latrice thinks.

No way in hell she'd say that shit out loud to her Haitian momma. As a matter-of-fact, thinking it is even a gamble.

"Mom, Nathan and I are not doing anything that could hurt Quincy or put his job in jeopardy."

"What the...? Girl, that's exactly what you're doing. How do you think his classmates are going to treat Quincy when they find out his mom is boning their teacher?"

"Mommy, please don't ever say 'boning.'"

"Stop being worried by my language and start paying attention to how this will affect your child. You're so concerned about Mark and Acacia. What about you?"

Latrice resents the implication that what she and

Nathan are doing is anywhere near as damaging as what Quincy's father is doing.

Her mother lets out a sigh and continues, "Latrice, I know it's been a while since you've been with a man. And I know what Mark did hurt you deeply. But, baby girl, please think about what you're doing. At least think about this man's job. He doesn't seem to be doing it."

"I am, Mom, I swear. He is thinking about his job. Nathan means a lot to me, and we are being careful. This isn't something we just did without thinking."

"I swear, I always knew you'd do something rebellious one day, but I thought it would be a tattoo or something. Just do me a favor?"

"Yes, Mom?"

"Think. Seriously think about how this will affect Quincy."

"I will."

"Thank you. We'll see you Saturday?"

"Yes, Mom."

"Good. Goodnight, baby."

"Goodnight, Mom."

Latrice hangs up and texts Thad.

LATRICE

Your days are numbered Thaddeus.

THAD

I'm guessing you talked to Mom.

LATRICE

Yep.

THAD

If it means anything, I told her under duress.

LATRICE

What duress?

THAD

She threatened to not make orange cake on Saturday.

LATRICE

You always thinking with your damn stomach.

THAD

When have you ever known me not to do that?

LATRICE

How did she even find out about Nathan?

THAD

She overheard me talking to Pop about it.

LATRICE

UGH!!! I'm going to get in my car, come to your house and slap the taste out your mouth.

THAD

Good luck with that. I'm out with Lance. We're having a guys night.

LATRICE

You've got a slap coming.

THAD

I love you, Trice.

LATRICE

You suck, T.

Latrice rolls her eyes and puts her phone away.

Sixteen

NATHAN

The kids arrive at school dressed in their various Halloween costumes. They wait at the front as usual, but this time, Nathan is hiding and watching them assemble. When they all arrive, he comes out dressed as T'Challa. All the kids cheer. Nathan does the "Wakanda forever" pose and says the famous words. The kids follow suit, then they walk to the classroom.

After they do their breathing ritual, Nathan greets them. "Happy Halloween, everybody."

Quincy, Eli and Ashleigh are dressed as the Three Musketeers. Some other costumes include Spider-Man, Cinderella, a Ninja Turtle and Darth Vader.

"Happy Halloween, Mr. Woodson," The kids respond.

"Okay, now if you remember, today is special. We'll have our lessons, but we'll be ending a little bit early for the Halloween parade."

The kids cheer some more. They are all super excited. Nathan is pretty hyped too. The parade includes a costume contest, and the winning classroom gets a movie day and pizza party in the auditorium in lieu of class on Friday.

Nathan holds up his hands to get the kids to settle down. He smiles at their enthusiasm. They aren't just excited for the day's activities. They're also happy because Nathan decided to switch up their usual schedule by having their English lesson first. A week ago, he assigned them the task of writing their own spooky stories to be shared in class. They've been working really hard on them, and a lot are eager to share.

"Alright. Let's get started. Who wants to go first?"

A few of the kids raise their hands. Nathan notices Ashleigh B. sink down in her chair. Hopefully, seeing a few of her classmates read their stories will make her more comfortable. Emily goes first. Her story features a Merlion, a creature found in folklore from Singapore. It's a fun cautionary tale with a happy ending and a few jump scares. That girl would have a successful career as a filmmaker.

Next up is Ashley G, Charlie and Spencer. Almost everyone has gone, including Quincy, who, like Emily, wrote a story from his Haitian roots. His story was about the Lougawou, evil spirits who come out at night and cause mischief. Nathan was happy to see so many of them use their heritage and culture for their story ideas. Eli, of course, chose to write a comedy rather than a scary one. Nathan only docked him a couple of points because the story was pretty fucking funny.

Brad is next. His is a story about a serial killer, which is pretty fucked up for an eight-year-old. Nathan was thinking they would write something that made their youthful imaginations shine through, not something one would hear on a true crime podcast, which is where Brad got his idea from. When he was done, the class gave him an obviously obligatory applause.

"Ashleigh B, you're up." Nathan gives her a warm smile.

She still looks scared to talk. She clings to her piece of paper as if her life depends on not letting it go.

"It's okay, Ash," Nathan hears Quincy say.

She looks at Quincy and smiles. Eli gives her a thumbs up.

Ashleigh giggles and begins her story about a coven of witches who curse a town so it's Halloween every day. When she's done, everyone cheers. Loudly. Ashleigh smiles so hard with tears in her eyes. Quincy hugs her. Nathan smiles. The bell rings.

"And that's first recess. You all go out and have fun. We'll be watching *It's the Great Pumpkin* with my boy, Charlie Brown, when you get back."

The kids let out a disappointed groan.

"We've been watching that since we were little, Mr. Woodson," Charlie complains.

"Yeah, can't we watch a horror movie? Like *Saw*?" Brad asks.

This kid really needs to see a fucking therapist.

"Look, ya'll, it's either *It's the Great Pumpkin* or we do math."

"*Great Pumpkin!*" all the kids cheer.

"That's what I thought." Nathan laughs.

Quincy hangs back and stands around his desk. Nathan notices.

"Everything okay, Quince?"

"Yeah, I'm good. It's just..."

"Just what, bud?"

"I wanted to tell you something."

Nathan remains calm, even though his heart is about to leap out of his chest. The thing at Latrice's house happened three weeks ago, and Quincy has seemed fine. But maybe he was waiting for the right time to bring it up. According to Latrice, Quincy didn't say anything, so they both figured that they were in the clear.

"Go ahead," Nathan says, keeping his voice even.

"Um, I just wanted to say that I like having you as a teacher. I've never had a Black teacher before, and it's pretty cool."

"Thank you, Quincy. It's been really cool having you as a student."

"Thanks." Quincy smiles as he heads out to recess.

~

LATRICE

Latrice brings a pitcher of margaritas and some leftover Halloween candy out to the backyard. The night has quieted down considerably. After she and Rachel took Quincy and Eli trick-or-treating, they stopped by a haunted house hosted by Jackson and Philip. The kids filled themselves with candy and are currently passed out on Quincy's bed. Latrice handed out a shitload of candy herself. Her house has always been a popular stop since she hands out full bars. Too tired to change out of her costume, Latrice—as Storm—takes a seat next to Rachel as the Scarlet Witch. Nay Nay aka Tina Turner and Drea the Nubian Queen join them.

"How was the firm Halloween party?" Latrice asks, pouring them each a drink.

"Go ahead, tell her Drea." Nadia shoots Drea a deadly look.

"What happened?" Rachel chuckles.

"I introduced your girl here to a very eligible, very fine lawyer, and Ms. Drea barely paid attention to anything the man had to say."

Drea rolls her eyes and finishes her drink.

Latrice refills it. "Start from the top," she says.

"He was boring. All he talked about were the recent cases he won." Drea explains.

Nadia jumps in. "Girl who cares? He was a sure thing for you to get some dick. I wasn't trying to introduce you to husband material."

"I told you, I don't want you to pull a Latrice and

Nathan on me. The last thing I need to have sex with a random stranger only for him to be Quincy's new soccer coach or something. No, thank you."

"Drea, Quincy doesn't play soccer." Latrice laughs.

"Yeah, but suppose he signs up next year and *bam*! The new coach is my weekly dick appointment."

"That wouldn't have happened with this dude," Nadia laments.

"Whatever, he was still boring."

"Fine. How about this? There's this dude I have in my Rolodex that could help you." Nadia wiggles her eyebrows.

"You mean like a sex worker?" Drea asks.

"No. I don't pay him. He's just a guy I know who likes to fuck and is really good at it. Just don't catch feelings for him cause he doesn't do that."

"So what, I just call him and we meet somewhere, he fucks my brains out and leaves?" Drea asks.

"Exactly."

"No, thank you. I mean, imagine having a man pop up and fuck me like crazy then leave while my neighbors might see? I mean, who does that?" Drea turns to Latrice and gives her a teasing smirk.

Latrice's face flushes as she thinks about how she and Nathan almost got caught doing what Drea described. She looks at Rachel, who looks at Drea. They both try not to laugh.

"What's so funny?" Nadia asks.

"What do you mean?" Latrice asks.

"I mean that look you, Drea and Rachel are giving each other." Nadia leans in like she's doing an interrogation. "What's going on?"

Rachel speaks up. "Tim ate me out so good this past weekend I passed out."

Latrice, Drea and Nadia stare at her in astonishment.

She continues, "He came home from work, took a shower and came out butt naked and then asked if I wanted my pussy eaten."

"Wow," Latrice says, giggling.

"Keep going, Rach." Drea grabs a peanut buttercup.

"The crazy part is that it happened the day before Mitch came to get Eli for the weekend, and that's when I realized Tim gets extra horny right before Mitch comes around. It's like his testosterone ramps up to eleven. Maybe it's because Mitch is still a huge jerk to Tim."

"Tim's marking his territory, sweetie." Latrice laughs.

"You think?" Rachel replies.

"Oh, hell yes. You see, Timmy boy knows that when Mitch shows up, he's gone smell them pheromones. And Tim wants to make sure Mitch knows whose pussy that now belongs to." Nadia says.

"Men are so ridiculous." Rachel laughs. "Have any of you ever been eaten so good you fainted before?"

"Yep. That's shit's amazing," Nadia says.

"Never," Drea pouts. She helps herself to a candy bar.

"I can now happily say I have." Latrice smirks.

"Go head, Nathan." Nadia grins. "You know you owe me for making that happen, right?"

"So you have mentioned dozens of times, Nay Nay." Latrice rolls her eyes.

The ladies continue to drink, laugh and talk. Around ten at night, Nadia and Drea share an Uber and head out. Rachel carries a passed out Eli and she heads to the door.

"When do you expect Tim home?"

"He's working today and tomorrow. Halloween week is always busy at the fire station."

Latrice angles herself to give Rachel a hug. "Thank you, Rach."

"What for?"

"I know you brought up Tim and Mitch because Nadia was getting nosy."

"Yeah, well, you were blushing so hard, and me and Drea were about to crack up. I wasn't sure if you wanted Nadia to know yet."

"No, I do not. I don't want to risk her big mouth ass telling Thad, then my parents finding out. Mom isn't exactly on board."

"If things keep getting serious with you two, Ms. Janet won't have a choice but to adjust. You're an adult."

"Thanks, Rachel. I'll see you tomorrow."

"Bright and early." Rachel readjusts Eli in her arms. "Jesus, when did he get so big? He's so fucking heavy."

"They aren't our little babies anymore."

"I know." Rachel struggles. "Yeah, I can't do this. Eli, wake up."

Eli blinks a few times. "What's happening?"

"We're going home, but you're going to have to walk. I'm not getting a hernia carrying you."

"Okay." Eli wakes up a little more and leans on his mom. "Bye, Auntie Tricey."

"Bye, baby."

Latrice watches Rachel and Eli walk out the door.

Latrice heads to her bedroom and removes her wig, makeup and costume, and takes a shower. She puts on her favorite pair of comfy pajamas and goes to Quincy's room. He's in his pj's sleeping soundly. She kisses him on the forehead, then goes back into her room. Latrice slides underneath the covers and dreams about what a future with Nathan would look like.

Seventeen

NATHAN

Nathan has a word problem on the board. It's a few minutes until recess, and he can tell the kids are getting antsy.

"Alright, my friends. Let's settle down. Take out a sheet of paper, and I want you all to answer the problem on the board. When you're done, hand it to me. Then you can go off to recess. Okay?"

"Okay," the kids all reply.

One by one, they answer the problem and hand their sheets to Nathan. Pretty soon, the only child left is Ashleigh B. She stares down at her paper and frowns. She gets up and hands the paper to Nathan before leaving the room quickly.

Nathan looks at her paper and is dismayed by what he sees.

Sorry Mr. Woodson. I don't know the answer. I'm really bad at math. I'm sorry I'm so dumb.

Dumb? This sounds like the work of bullies. Nathan needs to have a talk with Ashleigh's parents. If she is being bullied, then there's a good chance her parents don't know. Kids tend to keep stuff like this to themselves out of fear it will only get worse.

School lets out, and some kids are waiting for their parents, while others board the school bus. Nathan walks out and sees Ashleigh walking with her mother. They're headed to the Bear Burger parking lot. He jogs over.

"Hello, Ms. Bennett." Nathan smiles. "I'm Nathan Woodson, Ashleigh's teacher. I'm sorry we haven't gotten a chance to officially meet."

"Of course. I recognize you from the school newsletter. How can I help you?" Ms. Bennet replies. She's a beautiful golden-hued Black woman with green eyes, brown hair, a pouty mouth and a statuesque figure. Ashleigh favors her.

She tells Ashleigh to get in the car.

"I don't want to keep you, but I need to bring something to your attention."

"What's wrong?"

"I think Ashleigh might be getting bullied. She's been having trouble with math, and I'm looking into getting her a tutor. But it's been a slow process. Meanwhile, I gave the kids an assignment today, and this is what Ashleigh handed in."

Nathan takes a piece of paper out of his pocket and hands it to her. She unfolds the paper and reads it. She looks up at Nathan with sadness in her eyes.

"I suspect some kids have been teasing her. This isn't something a child comes up with on their own."

"Thank you for telling me."

"It's my pleasure. I'm going to talk to Principal Tanaka about having a student from the middle school down the street come by the class and help Ashleigh during our math period. They offer electives to the kids that involve tutoring elementary school kids. I'm hoping we can come up with a plan to get help for Ashleigh. "

"If you need me to sign off on anything, let me know."

"Will do."

"Now if you'll excuse me, I have to get Miss Ashleigh home and get to my afternoon job."

"Ms. Bennett, you have two jobs?"

"Yes, I have a full-time job from six to two, then I get Ashleigh and drop her off at home before heading to my next job from four to eleven. Her dad is usually home by five and makes her dinner. He works twelve-hour shifts."

"That sounds exhausting."

Ms. Bennett gives Nathan a weak smile. "It is, but the schools in our neighborhood aren't very good, and my husband and I want what's best for Ashleigh. Attending Glen Oak will help her tremendously."

Ms. Bennett looks over at her daughter and smiles.

"As much as we adults like to tell children that their

sparkling personalities are enough to attract friends, you and I both know that's not true. Ashleigh has never really felt like she belongs here due to where we live. She sees these kids with their cell phones, expensive clothes and huge houses and doesn't feel like she can compete. My husband and I work so she can feel like she belongs, even if it's just because of the shoes and clothes she has. Is it shallow? Maybe, but it keeps her from feeling like more of an outsider. To find out she's being bullied anyway..." Ms. Bennett trails off.

Nathan's heart aches for this woman, her husband and Ashleigh. Unfortunately, she's right. At Glen Oak, like most schools, image is everything. It's the main reason Ms. Kopel is as insufferable as she is. Popularity is often rated by what you have rather than who you are.

Nathan is reminded of one of his earliest memories at a new school. He had just been placed at Momma's, and when he arrived at school, he was still getting used to his new family. He had on some of Leon's hand-me-downs, and he got severely roasted the entire day. His glasses didn't help. He saw all the other kids in Jordans and Rocawear, and he desperately wanted to fit in.

Upon learning about Ashleigh's insecurities with math and now her discomfort being around all these rich kids, Nathan's even more determined to make her feel at ease. He sees a lot of himself in her.

Nathan looks at Ms. Bennett with a strong resolve. "I will get Ashleigh the help she needs. I promise."

Ms. Bennett smiles. "Thank you."

Nathan looks over at Ashleigh in the back seat and smiles at her. She smiles back. He makes the gesture for her to roll down her window, and she does.

"Hey, Ashleigh." Nathan cheerfully grins at her.

"Hi, Mr. Woodson." She smiles back.

"I want you to do me a favor, okay?"

"Okay."

"I want you to repeat after me."

"Okay."

"I'm a big bright, shining star, and no one can dim my light."

"I'm a big bright, shining star, and no one can dim my light."

"Good. I want you to tell yourself that anytime someone tries to make you feel bad about yourself. Anytime they try to make you feel small. No matter who it is. Okay?"

"Okay."

"Thank you."

Nathan nods at Ms. Bennett and makes his way back into the school.

It's 9 p.m. and Nathan is lying on his couch refamiliarizing himself with *Tales of a Fourth Grade Nothing*. With the kids getting ready to read the Judy Blume classic for English, he wanted to get a head start on reading it. Especially since it's been twenty years since he last read it.

"I forgot how annoying Fudge is," Nathan mumbles to himself.

His phone buzzes. It's Latrice calling on FaceTime. Seeing her name flash across his screen makes him smile. He sits up and puts the book down.

"Hi, Lala."

"Hey, so I've been reluctant to share this but...my mom knows about us."

"And how did that come to pass? Wait, did your parents see me leave?"

"No, Mr. Flush, they didn't."

Nathan laughs. "Mr. Flush?"

"Yep, that's your new nickname."

"I don't think I like it."

"Too bad." Latrice giggles.

"C'mon I gave you 'Lala.' That's sexy. I can't get stuck with Mr. Flush."

"Then maybe don't do something silly like flushing a toilet when my parents are here, alerting them that you're in my room. Be sure to remember that the next time you come over."

"So there's going to be a next time?"

"As soon as I can figure out how to pull that off, of course."

Nathan smiles. "How was your day?"

"Busy. Yours?"

"Also busy, but I had a bit of a breakthrough with a kid in my class. That was rewarding."

"I'm happy to hear that. Have you started making teacher friends yet?"

"Not yet."

"Nathan." Latrice says in a playfully nagging tone.

She can't pull off nagging to save her life. Instead, she just sounds sexy as hell.

"I will. I promise."

Nathan hears a buzzing sound.

"Was that your phone?" he asks.

"Yep, it's Nay Nay. She's a little stressed with work."

"What does Nadia do anyway?"

"She's a divorce lawyer. Runs her own firm. I'm convinced she became an attorney because she felt compelled to use her powers of persuasion to get paid," she says.

"At five hundred dollars per hour?" Nathan adds.

"Oh, honey, Nay Nay charges nine hundred."

"Damn, she must be really good."

"She is. Though she's been overwhelmed lately."

"Why is that?"

"She's in need of a new assistant and hasn't had much luck finding one."

"I have no doubt she'll succeed. Nadia doesn't strike me as the type to take defeat lightly, no matter what the issue is."

"You would be correct, sir."

Nathan chuckles. "What does Thad do?"

"He owns and operates a chain of barbershops. They're called *We Cut Heads.*"

Holy shit! Thad basically owns the Black version of Supercuts. Okay, maybe not Supercuts, but there are numerous locations of his shop all over Southern California.

"That's fucking cool, Lala. You and your family are so accomplished. I can only imagine what Quincy's future holds."

"Okay, speaking as Quincy's teacher and not the man I'm seeing, he's one of the best kids in your class, isn't he?"

"Quincy is an exceptional child."

"That's all you're going to give me?"

"Can't appear to show favoritism."

"Nathan, it's just me and you talking."

"I know, but if I let myself pick favorites, it'll inevitably bleed into how I treat them. I care about the kids too much to do that."

"Wow."

"What?"

"After Mark, it's refreshing to be with a man who has so much integrity."

"Thank you."

"I was just kidding, by the way."

"So if I said that Quincy was my absolute favorite and my best student, you wouldn't have been pleased to hear that?"

Latrice stares at him, not responding as he smirks at her.

"What did you have for dinner tonight?" she asks, blatantly changing the subject.

"That was very transparent."

"Whatever. What did you eat?"

"There's a Mexican joint I like to hit up on the way home. I got a carne asada burrito."

"That sounds good. We'll have to go there sometime."

"Definitely."

"How about this? Once school is over and we've finally talked to Quincy, we all go there for dinner. How does that sound?"

Nathan smiles widely. Hearing Latrice talk about their future means so much to him. It gives him hope that she's falling for him too. When he told her he was falling for her and she didn't say it back, it hurt, but he didn't want to say anything to upset her. He hadn't brought it up since. He feels safe he can tell her again.

It's not lost on him how huge it is that she's thinking about when to tell Quincy. She's willing to tell him about them. She once told him during one of their calls that a few of the men she dated hinted at meeting her son—they didn't know his name—and when that happened, she'd end things soon after.

"That sounds great. I can't wait for that day, Lala."

"Me too."

"What did your mom have to say about us?" Nathan asks.

"She's not thrilled that I'm dating Quincy's teacher."

"I'm not surprised. Pushback is to be expected from parents."

"What do you think your mom will say?"

"She was so happy when I told her I met a woman. I'm not sure she'd care."

"Will I be the first woman you've dated that she'll ever meet?"

"No, I've introduced her to women before, but it never went past the initial introduction for a lot of them."

"Nobody ever met any of the men I've dated, and now everyone but my parents have met you."

Nathan laughs. Latrice joins him.

These long talks have breathed so much new life into Nathan. The only disadvantage is she's not here with him. He would give anything to feel her smooth skin, to kiss her softly while making her come over and over. *Shit!*

"What are you wearing, Lala?"

"What in the non sequitur?" She chuckles.

"I'm mostly seeing your face. I can't see your body. So I need you to describe it to me."

Latrice smiles sweetly. When she gets embarrassed like this, it makes Nathan want to bend her over and fuck the shit out of her. His dick even harder at the thought.

"I'm wearing a plain black T-shirt and boy shorts."

Nathan's dick might break. There's no way he can be *this* hard.

"What about you, Mr. Woodson? What are you wearing?"

"I'm wearing boxers."

"And?"

"And that's it."

"Can you send me a picture?"

Nathan takes his dick out and takes a picture of himself from the chest down. He sends it and eagerly awaits her response.

Latrice giggles. "I look forward to you nutting down my throat."

"Fuck, Latrice. You gon' make me nut right now."

"If you do, I want to see it."

"Say less."

Nathan positions his phone so that all of him can be seen. He closes his eyes and pictures Latrice naked. Her nipples are hard, her pussy soaking wet. She turns around and bends over, showing him that incredible, fat ass and a view of her sweet pussy from behind. He strokes himself faster. All of his senses are on fire. He needs to chill or else he'll come before she does.

"Nathan," Latrice whimpers.

Nathan fucks his hand harder. Latrice has to be careful saying his name like that. He's liable to hop in his car and go straight to her house. Neighbors be damned. A buzzing sound comes from Latrice's side. At first, he curses, thinking it's Nay Nay, but when Latrice begins to moan, he knows it's not her phone. The buzzing gets louder. Nathan fucks his hand faster.

"Fuck, Lala!"

"Nathan!"

Her moan is so hoarse he can barely hear her.

"Lala, please. Tell me you're close."

"I am. I'm so close. I'm so... fuck! Nathan," she cries.

"Argh!" His nut spills down his hands and onto his couch.

"Goddamn, Nathan."

"I know, Lala."

"I . . . I have to sleep now." Latrice yawns.

"Yeah, me too." Nathan is spent.

He's never come that hard from jerking off. His eyes are heavy.

"Goodnight, Nathan."

"Goodnight, Lala. I love you."

Eighteen

NATHAN

athan sits in his car and takes some deep breaths. Momma called him during his lunch break and told him the great news. Leon's newest venture to expand Chomp is rolling out sooner than expected. In a few months, Chomp Groceries will be available for iPhone users and for Android users by this summer. Momma insisted that the family get together and celebrate. Having to sit through an evening of Leon being an ass is not what he had in mind. His plans to get Latrice alone and naked have been thwarted again, so he's more than a little grumpy. He overheard Quincy inviting Ashleigh to come to the movies with him and Eli after school. Thad's taking them. Nathan wanted to surprise Latrice by stopping at her boutique and taking her somewhere special.

He gets out of the car and can hear Momma and Amber laughing.

"Nathaniel, baby. You're here." Momma stands up.

"What took you so long?" Leon asks in a nasty tone.

"Leon," Momma says gently.

What the fuck is his problem?

Nathan's only twenty minutes late, and dinner isn't even on the table yet.

"I had assignments to grade," Nathan explains.

"See now, if you would come and work for me, you'd be off by five and able to live your life."

"So you've said," Nathan says flatly.

"It's not too late, Nate. You can have a 401k, great benefits." Leon starts in on him.

"I'm fine where I am. I like my job, and I enjoy teaching."

There's some bite in Nathan's tone. He is sick of having this same fucking conversation, and he doesn't want to have it anymore. Leon gets the hint. There's an awkward silence in the room that gets disrupted by Tyler and Shellie when they enter.

"Uncle Nate!" Tyler runs up to him and gives him a hug.

Nathan smiles and hugs Tyler tightly. He hugs Shellie next and picks her up. She squeals. Even though Tyler is ten and Shellie is nine, they still get super excited to see Nathan, just like they did when they were toddlers. He loves it and relaxes a little.

"Nathan, tell everybody about your new lady friend," Momma requests.

The kids and Amber all look at him with happy and surprised expressions. Leon looks annoyed.

"Uncle Nate, you have a girlfriend?" Shellie asks.

"Yeah. I do." Nathan smiles.

"What's her name?" Amber asks.

"Latrice."

"Where did you meet?" Shellie asks.

"At a restaurant."

"When do we get to meet her?" Momma asks.

"Probably not until the end of the school year."

"Why?"

"Not long after we met at Cork & Marble, I found out she's a parent at the school."

"Really?" Amber asks.

"Yeah, so we're going to wait until the school year is over before going public."

Leon gives him a peculiar look. "Why? It's not like you're teaching her kid, are you?"

"Yes, her son is one of my students," Nathan says, sounding defensive.

"Oh. Nathaniel, baby, are you sure that's wise?" Momma asks.

"It's fine, Momma. A teacher can't get fired for dating a parent."

"Even so, you don't see how inappropriate that is?" Leon argues.

Nathan's jaw ticks. He does not have the patience to deal with Leon's bullshit right now.

The timer on the oven goes off, and Momma Ernie

gets up quickly and retreats to the kitchen to get the roast out of the oven. She places it on a serving platter and uses the veggies—potatoes, carrots, string beans and celery—as a garnish around the meat. She takes the salad out of the fridge and hands it to Amber, who places it on the table. Momma Ernie puts the roast near the salad and hands the serving utensils to Leon, who slices the roast.

Nathan watches his mother's movements. He knows she's hoping that if she puts the food out, all the focus will shift toward eating. Whenever Leon gets on his nonsense, she tries little tricks to diffuse it. Nathan takes her hand and squeezes it, letting her know he appreciates the effort. Too bad it didn't work.

"What kind of a mother fools around with her kid's teacher?" Leon says in disgust.

Nathan checks his temper, not wanting to be disrespectful in front of his mother or Leon's kids, but he also can't sit back and let him bad-mouth Latrice.

"Latrice is an amazing mother."

"Stop getting defensive, Nate. It was a simple question."

"It wasn't a question. You were being judgmental."

"Somebody should be. What's with all these dumbass decisions you've been making for years?"

"Leon, that's enough," Momma Ernie warns.

"How am I the bad guy here? He refuses to get a job that will keep him financially stable, and now he's doing something that could jeopardize the low-paying job he has and mess up some poor kid."

"I already told you my job isn't in jeopardy, and we plan to tell Quincy together *after* the school year is over. Meanwhile, we've been playing it safe."

Except for that one time with her parents, but Leon's annoying ass doesn't need to know that.

"And if her kid isn't okay with ya'll being together, then what?" Leon asks.

"Why does this matter so much to you?" Nathan asks.

"Why does this matter so *little* to you? I swear, Nate, it's like you don't take your future seriously at all."

"Can we please just have a nice dinner?" Momma Ernie says, exasperation flowing through her tone. "We're supposed to be celebrating."

"And we were until Nate brought all the focus on him as usual," Leon complains.

Nathan has had it. "Oh, my god! That's what it's always about, isn't it Lee? You are thirty-one years old, and you're still salty that you have to share our mother with me."

"Nathan," his mother pleads.

"No, no. I'm done, Momma. I'm done listening to Leon judge me and my life." Nathan gets up and turns his attention to Leon. "Since you are, and always have been, so pissed at my presence, I'll go. That way you can have mommy all to yourself. Since that's what you've always wanted."

"Nathan, baby. Please." his mother gets up.

"I'm sorry, Momma. I can't even be in the same room with him anymore."

Nathan hurries out of the door, gets in his car and drives off.

He drives around aimlessly. His phone hasn't stopped blowing up since he left. Momma Ernie keeps calling while Leon keeps sending him text after text.

LEON

Nate, you're being ridiculous.

I hope you're happy. Momma's really upset with me.

I was just being honest. It's not my fault you're so sensitive.

Nathan arrives at Mtindo. He leans his head on the steering wheel and lets in a deep breath. He is sorry for the uncomfortable position he's put his mother in. She only has two children. It can't be easy when they're currently going to war with one another, but Nathan's through with Leon's attitude. As much as he wishes they had a real brotherly bond, that just isn't in the cards.

There's a knock on the passenger side window. Nathan looks up and sees Latrice. He gets out of the car, hugs her and gives her a kiss. She takes his hand, and he follows her into the store. He gives Ingrid a quick wave before they go into Latrice's office.

"Hey." He smiles.

Nathan may be in a bad headspace, but seeing her face always helps.

His smile can't hide his feelings. Latrice looks like she can tell something is off as she cups his face in her hand.

"Hey, Nathan. What's wrong?"

"I was at my mother's, and me and Leon got into an argument. Again. So I left."

"What did you argue about?"

"You. My life. You being in my life."

"Oh."

"He was talking shit about me dating a student's parent. It was just another excuse for him to talk shit about my life."

"I'm sorry."

"It's fine. He and I just can't be around each other anymore."

"Whoa, you sure you want to take things that far?"

"What do you mean?"

"He is your only sibling, Nathan. And you're supposed to be adding more people into your circle, not taking any away. Talk to him. Offer an olive branch and see where it takes you."

Nathan frowns. He's really not in the mood to hear this. Mainly because he knows she's right, but he's choosing to stand ten toes in his stubborn decision. He has no interest in hearing logic right now.

"I think I should go."

"Seriously?" Now Latrice is frowning.

"Yeah, look, I'm sorry, but I'm not interested in having a relationship with Leon anymore. And hearing that I have to be the bigger man when I always am isn't improving my mood."

"Okay, fine."

"I'll talk to you later."

"Sure."

Nathan knows he's fucking up things with Latrice, but he can't help it. He came here hoping she'd have his back. She knows how things are between him and Leon, but is looking at this through the point of view of someone with a good relationship with their siblings. She couldn't possibly get where he's coming from.

Nathan leaves her office, giving Ingrid a rushed goodbye.

Nineteen

LATRICE

L atrice goes through the usual routine she's been doing for the past week. She wakes up, gets ready, gets Quincy up, makes breakfast and drops him off at school. She then goes to work, picks Quincy up and goes home. There have been no late-night phone calls with her and Nathan. She even avoided looking at him as he stands in front of the school waiting for the kids in the morning.

"Is everything okay, Mom?" Quincy asks as they pull up in front of the school.

"Yeah, sweetie. Everything's fine. Why?"

"You just seem sad."

"Oh, um…"

Someone honks behind them.

"You better go, Quince."

"Okay. Are you sure everything is okay, Mom?"

"I'm sure, honey."

Quincy smiles at her and hops out of the car. Latrice puts on a brave face, but she isn't sure if everything is okay. She and Nathan are clearly avoiding each other. She wants to give him space, then maybe they can try to fix things when they both cool down.

Latrice heads to the boutique. She has a ten o'clock with Katrina Spencer, a designer who is showing her newest collection exclusively to them.

The day goes swimmingly. Katrina's designs are amazing. Latrice knows all the A-list stars will be clamoring for them.

She finishes her workday and picks up Quincy. They stop at the grocery store to pick up some more food for the week. Quincy's in the middle of yet another growth spurt, so their food supply has gotten low.

She and Quincy laugh and joke as she adds more items into the cart. He runs off to get some pancake mix.

Latrice hears giggling. She looks up and sees a beautiful Black couple smiling and kissing while standing in line. Their adorable kids, a boy and a girl, are standing close by, smiling lovingly at their parents. Latrice pictures her and Nathan with Quincy, being able to love each other freely. She needs to call him.

Quincy comes back, and Latrice fixes her face. "Ready to go, kiddo?"

"Yep."

At exactly nine o'clock, Latrice calls Nathan via FaceTime.

"Hi, Lala," Nathan answers.

He's calling her by her nickname. That's a good sign. His voice sounds melodic and forlorn, while sadness is etched on his face. For a second, Latrice forgets to reply.

"Hi, Nathan."

"I'm sorry," they say at the same time.

They look at each other and chuckle at their mutual faux pas.

"You go first," Latrice says.

"I am so sorry, Latrice. You were just trying to offer me another perspective on how I should approach my brother, and I snapped at you. I was already in my feelings over our argument. I shouldn't have pushed you away. This week, seeing you avoid looking at me—"

Shit. He noticed.

"I'm sorry, Nathan. It wasn't really anger. It was hard to look at you knowing you were mad at me."

"That's just it. I was upset at your words, not you. I should have made that clear. I'm sorry, Lala. I love you."

"I love you too."

He gives her a look that tells her hearing those words have a healing effect on him. She recognizes it because she feels it too.

"Have you spoken to your mother?"

"Yes. She keeps trying to get me to call Leon. I'm just not ready. I doubt Leon wants to talk to me anyway. One of the texts he sent after I left accused me of being Momma's favorite."

Latrice lets out a humorless chuckle. "He should talk to Drea."

"Why?"

"She actually is the least favorite child. What your mother is doing doesn't seem like favoritism. She's just trying to find a middle ground between her two boys. Leon seems to be way more loved than Drea is."

"Wait, your ex-husband is the favorite child? The egotistical cheater?"

"Yep."

"How is that possible? I mean, I only met Drea that one time, but she's a sweetheart."

"She really is."

"Then how the hell is he the favorite?"

Latrice giggles, relieved that she and Nathan are on good terms.

"How else? Misogyny. Mark was their firstborn after years of trying, so he was automatically the golden child. Add to that Drea being an 'oops' baby and Mark being a momma's boy."

Nathan shakes his head. "It's like peeling an onion with that nigga."

They share a laugh. Soon, they're both quiet. Nathan looks like he's deep in thought.

"What's going on in that head of yours, Mr. Woodson?"

"Just trying to figure out how to approach Leon—if I decide to try and fix things. I'd like to get past this whole thing with him and try to really be brothers, but I'm not sure it's possible."

"Nathan, of course it is. You're family. Just talk to him."

"Um."

"Only when you're ready, though." She smiles.

"Thank you."

He gazes at Latrice with a smoldering look in his eyes. "You are a goddamn goddess."

"Nathan," Latrice looks away, embarrassed.

"Look at me."

She raises her eyes to his. Nathan stares at her. Latrice feels exposed as he drinks in every part of her.

"Do you have any clue how much I crave you?" he whispers. "When I was fifteen, we went on a class field trip to an art museum that displayed paintings and sculptures from all over the diaspora, and I spent damn near the entire day in wonder as I gazed upon a painting of Yemayá, the ocean mother goddess in Santería."

"My Haitian grandmother told me stories about her," Latrice says in a dreamy voice.

"You're basically her doppelgänger. Her skin is dark, her body the definition of heaven, and her power." Nathan lets out a sigh. "It was evident, even through a simple canvas with paint. My breath was taken. I never felt that way again until I saw you walk into Cork & Marble. You are a goddess, Latrice."

Latrice is speechless. *How? How does he manage to say such romantic and sexy things?*

"Why are you not here so I can suck your dick?"

"I will remedy that soon."

She never wants to be away from this man. He said he craves her, but she yearns for him.

~

Latrice and Quincy enter her parents' house. Quincy gives his grandfather a hug. Thad and Nadia are already here. They're helping to set the table. Everyone has a specific role. Her father sits in his chair and waits to hear that dinner is ready while everyone else prepares the meal and gets the dinner table set. It's been that way since the three of them were kids. Latrice brought her wings already prepared. She wanted to limit time in the kitchen with her mother. She doesn't feel like being given another lecture. Something her mother hasn't stopped doing since the initial phone call about her and Nathan.

"Baby, go help grandma in the kitchen while I say hi to grandpa," Latrice tells Quincy.

"Yes, Mom."

Quincy heads to the kitchen. Latrice smiles as she hears her mother and siblings greet him.

"Hey, Dad," Latrice greets her father with a kiss on the cheek.

"Hey, Tricey." Her father smiles. "Are you still messing around with that young buck?"

"Yes, and that reminds me, I need to kill your son."

Earl laughs. "Don't be too hard on him. Wasn't his fault your momma was eavesdropping."

"What do you think?"

"About what, baby?"

"About me seeing Quincy's teacher."

"I think you're an intelligent woman and a damn good mother. You wouldn't be doing something like this if you knew it was going to hurt your son."

Latrice thinks over her father's words. The truth is, she's not one hundred percent sure if this would hurt Quincy. Her instincts tell her it wouldn't, based on how he talks about Nathan, but that's as his teacher. Would things be different when she and Nathan reveal they are a couple?

"Dinner's ready!" Her mother calls out.

Latrice and Earl make their way to the dinner table. Latrice places the chicken wings with the rest of the food. Dinner consist of her wings, Nay Nay's oxtails, Thad's pulled pork, scalloped potatoes, butter rolls, mixed greens with cherry tomatoes and Broccolini. Everyone takes their seat.

"Let's bow our heads and say thanks," Her father says.

The family joins hands and bows their heads.

"Thank you, Lord, for allowing our family to join together, and we thank you for this meal prepared by my beautiful wife and children. We give thanks for all that you have blessed us with and ask that you continue to keep us safe, happy and healthy. In Jesus' name, amen."

"Amen," the family replies.

Latrice makes a plate for Quincy, then herself.

"Latrice, have you given any more thought to what we've discussed?" Her mother asks.

"Yes, Mom. I have."

"And?"

"And I'm going to continue with my plans."

Nadia nudges Latrice playfully and smiles at her.

"Why am I not surprised that you're encouraging this, Nay Nay?" Her mother responds.

"Momma, Latrice is just having some fun."

"What she's doing is irresponsible and dangerous." Her mother adds some salad to her plate.

"What's everyone talking about?" Quincy asks.

"Well, baby, your mother wants to . . . go bungee jumping. And I don't think it's a good idea," Her mother explains quickly.

Bungee jumping? That's the best she could come up with?

"Cool, Mom! I think you should do it," Quincy says, filled with excitement.

Hopefully, he sounds this excited when he learns about her and Nathan.

"See, Momma? Quincy's all for it," Nadia argues.

"That's because he's only eight and doesn't know any better," Her mother retorts.

Thad leans over and whispers to Latrice, "Are we still

talking about dude from Quincy's school, or are you actually going bungee jumping?"

Latrice gives him a look that says, "What do you think?"

"Mom, I have given this a lot of thought, and I have talked things over with my, uh, bungee instructor. And I am good with my decision."

"Fine. I won't say another word." Her mother cuts into a piece of meat.

Everyone eats silently until her mother speaks up again.

"I will just say this . . ."

"Janet, baby, didn't you just say you weren't going to say another word?" Earl pipes up.

"Latrice has always been responsible." Her mother looks at Latrice and pleads with her. "I just don't understand why you would want to do something so reckless."

Latrice looks at her warmly. "Mom, bungee jumping makes me feel alive. It's been incredible. I really enjoy the time I spend doing it. It makes me happier than I've felt in years."

Latrice feels tears sting her eyes.

"Wow, Mom. You make bungee jumping sound really cool," Quincy says.

"It sounds like you love it," Her mother says.

"I do. I really do." Latrice wipes her eyes.

"Then just be careful. And make sure you don't get hurt," Her mother says softly.

"I won't. My bungee instructor is really amazing. I promise."

The family resumes having dinner. Latrice catches Nadia's eye. She smiles at her and mouths, "You're in love," in a teasing manner that makes Thad chuckle. Latrice rolls her eyes at her siblings and wonders how she's going to tell Quincy.

Twenty

NATHAN

It's Monday morning, and the hustle and bustle of the kids arriving never gets old. It's Thanksgiving week, and Nathan has made plans to give the kids a breather before their break. It's mainly going to be spent watching movies and making Thanksgiving arts and crafts, culminating in a class party on Wednesday. He stands in front of the school like he does every morning, ready to greet the kids, when he sees Ashleigh crying as she gets off the school bus. He approaches her and offers his hand. She takes it and they go into the school. Once inside, she sits on the floor in the hallway with her head down, crying into her hands.

Nathan kneels and puts his arm around her. "Ashleigh, what's wrong?"

"A few of the kids were making fun of me. They called me stupid because I'm not good at math." She cries.

Nathan has been working with Ashleigh. She tends to get nervous when he calls on her. He will walk through the problem with her until she understands and she is slowly getting better. Kids teasing her is just going to stifle her progress.

He takes Ashleigh's hand and gives it a squeeze. "Ashleigh, look at me. What do we say when someone makes us feel small?"

"I'm. I'm a big..." Ashleigh looks up at Nathan, her big green eyes filled with sadness. She sniffles.

"Go on."

"I'm a big bright, shining star, and no one can dim my light."

Nathan hands her a tissue. He always has a box on his desk and a travel pack in his pocket ever since he started working with little ones. Ashleigh takes it and wipes away her tears.

"Very good. Let me know which kids were making fun of you, and I'll take care of it."

"Okay," Ashleigh B. replies.

Some teachers are in the hall greeting their arriving kids, respectively. Quincy comes in with his dad.

I wonder if we're going to hear horns blaring at any second.

Quincy approaches them. "Ashleigh, are you okay?"

Nathan smiles at Quincy. His deep concern for his friend is admirable.

"Quincy, your teacher is handling this. Go to class," Mark orders.

"I just want to make sure Ashleigh's okay," Quincy argues.

"I said your teacher is handling it. Besides, this isn't any of your concern. Now go to class," Mark replies.

Well, it's clear which parent Quincy got his empathy from.

Quincy heads inside.

Mark addresses Ashleigh, "Look, sweetie, I'm sorry for whatever it is you're dealing with, but I need to speak to him." He points to Nathan.

Did this motherfucker just dismiss my student?

Nathan looks at Ashleigh, who is much calmer and just as confused as he is.

"Ashleigh, head in. We'll talk later."

"Okay, Mr. Woodson."

Nathan turns his attention to Mark. "Is there a problem, Mr. Johnson?"

"Yes, there is. I'm going to need you to stop fucking my ex-wife."

Nathan is shocked as hell but keeps his composure. He certainly didn't see this coming. The plan was to let everyone else who is family or friends know after Quincy. This definitely throws a wrench into their plan. Thankfully, Nathan's the only one who heard Mark. All the teachers went into their classrooms. It's just the two of them.

"I don't know what you're talking about," Nathan replies.

Mark walks closer. The two look like opponents getting ready to duke it out in a ring.

"I think you do," Mark says.

"Okay. I think we've had enough testosterone for the morning," Rachel cuts in.

Nathan and Mark turn to see Rachel and Dana watching them. Nathan didn't even realize they were standing there. Thankfully Brad and Eli enter after Mark's demand about Nathan and Latrice. Mark shoots Nathan another dirty look before he leaves.

Dana has her phone out and filmed the whole interaction. Nathan approaches her.

"Please delete that, Ms. Kopel."

She grins at Nathan like he's a snack. He resists the urge to roll his eyes.

"If Latrice is getting special treatment, then people have the right to know."

"I don't know what Mr. Johnson thinks is the nature of my interactions with Ms. Richardson, nor do I care, because he's clearly mistaken."

"Is that so?" Dana replies smugly.

"Yes, it is," Nathan warns.

"Kids, go inside," Rachel chimes in.

Eli and Brad obey. Rachel snatches Dana's phone from her hand.

"Hey, give that back!" Dana demands.

"Dana, I have put up with your bullshit for years for your son's sake, but Latrice is my friend. If you post the footage anywhere online or breathe a word of what you think you know, I'll make sure you and your family will be pariahs at Glen Oak." Rachel's voice is calm, but her tone is venomous.

Dana actually looks nervous.

Rachel continues, "You know what that means, don't you? No more invitations to anything, and no one coming to Brad's Fourth of July pool party. You and I both know I can do that. Delete the footage, and keep your mouth shut."

Nathan can't believe his eyes when he sees Dana nod her head, bending to Rachel's demand. Rachel hands her back her phone and Dana deletes the video, then leaves.

"You can't appeal to any decency when Dana doesn't have any. You got to go for the jugular. That's the only language folks like her and Mark speak." Rachel smiles and pats him on the shoulder as she heads out.

"Good to know," Nathan says to himself and goes into the classroom.

After school, Nathan gathers his belongings and heads toward the door when he sees Greg heading out. He hasn't put in much effort to make more friends, and given the shock of this morning, he could use a drink and someone to talk to. Nathan had a hell of a time focusing today. He considered calling in a last-minute sub and going home early. The whole day, he was trying to figure out how Mark found out about him and Latrice.

The bright side of the day came when Ashleigh told Nathan who the culprits from this morning were. They're three fifth-grade girls she rides the bus with.

Nathan got their names and brought Ashleigh to Principal Tanaka's office. The fifth graders' parents will be notified.

Nathan catches up to Greg. "Hey."

"Hey." Greg smiles. "I heard you had some kind of run-in with a parent today. How you holding up?"

Nathan rolls his eyes. "Yep, it happened this morning. I could use a drink."

"I'll bet."

"Was thinking about getting a beer. You want to join me?"

Greg looks surprised. "Yeah, sure. I know the perfect spot we can go to."

"Cool."

Twenty-five minutes later, they're walking into a gastro brewery where the decor looks like an old English pub. Nathan and Greg take a seat in a booth.

"I'm glad you asked to hang out," Greg comments.

"Yeah, me too. I've been meaning to do so sooner, but—"

"It's no problem. The beginning of the school year is a lot, especially for a first-timer."

"Exactly. I'm glad you get it."

"Everyone in this bar gets it."

"What do you mean?"

"Let me be the first to welcome you to the Fat Brew Bar and Grill. There are cop bars, and there are firemen bars. This here, Nathan, is a teacher's bar. Over there," Greg points to a nearby booth. "are the hard-working faculty at Glen Oak High. Over at the table on the left are the fine folks at Mountain Ridge Elementary. In the back is Woodcrest Middle School. And in the corner are the teachers of Our Lady of Fatima, an all-girl's K through twelve."

"Wow. And you guys come here every day after school?"

"Not every day, just whenever we have a stressful, mind-numbing day filled with low test scores and aggravating parents."

"So basically, every day?" Nathan laughs.

"Yeah, pretty much," Greg joins him.

A waitress comes by to take their orders. She looks sweet, with bright red hair and freckles sprinkled all over her nose and cheeks.

"Hey, Greg! You brought a friend. Hello, and welcome to Fat Brew Bar and Grill. What can I get you?"

"Amy, this is Nathan, the newest addition to the Glen Oak faculty."

"Welcome, Nathan. Happy to have you."

"Thank you."

"What will you be having?"

"I'll defer to Greg."

"We'll have two Dank Monkeys." Greg turns to Nathan. "It's a ridiculous name, but it's a really good beer."

"Sounds good."

"Can I get you guys anything to eat?" Amy asks.

"The burgers here are really good," Greg suggests.

"Works for me."

"Two cheeseburgers, Amy."

"How do you want your burgers cooked, and what kind of cheese would you guys like?"

"I'll have mine well with cheddar," Nathan says.

"Medium with American, please," Greg replies.

"Great. I'll be right back with your beers."

"Thank you, Amy," Greg says.

Nathan smiles. "Thank you."

"So what happened today? I heard someone mention Dana Kopel trying to film you."

Shit! Nathan has no doubt Dana went running her mouth to someone. It looks like Rachel's threat didn't work. As if this whole thing with Mark knowing wasn't enough, God knows what Dana told people and who she told.

"This morning, I had a run-in with a student's dad."

Greg shakes his head. "Confrontational parents just make our job even harder."

"They never bother to pay attention to the damage they're doing, and they don't care. And Quincy's dad was just..."

"Just what?" Greg inquires.

Nathan wants to be careful that he doesn't get too personal about his interaction with Mark. He has to tread lightly. Granted, a number of people already know about his relationship with Latrice, but none of those people are from the school. If he said what he was really feeling—that Mark is a worthless piece of shit who fucked up his marriage and has no right to demand Nathan stop seeing Latrice—that, of course, would open up a whole can of worms.

"Just as entitled as the rest of them."

"I bet he's an absent parent too."

Nathan's tempted to tell him he hit the nail on the head, but he keeps quiet.

Greg continues, "The parents who ignore their kids are the worst. Their children just want their attention, and when they don't get it, they, of course, use us as stand-ins only for those parents to accuse us of overstepping."

"That's basically what happened."

Granted, the so-called overstepping involved Latrice, not Quincy.

Amy drops off their beers. Nathan and Greg toast.

"To low wage paying, thankless jobs that cause large amounts of stress but give us purpose and fulfillment," Greg says.

"Here, here." Nathan grins.

Nathan's mind wanders back to Ashleigh. Between her academic struggles and her desperation to fit in, the poor girl has to be filled with anxiety. Her folks having to work long hours isn't helpful at all. If only there was... Nathan thinks for a second and smiles. His eyes light up.

"Nadia," he says to himself.

That's what he'll do. He will talk to Ms. Bennett and ask her if she would be interested in the assistant position at Nadia's firm. First, he needs to find out specifics like salary and benefits. Nathan pulls out his phone.

"What are you doing?" Greg asks.

"I have an idea." Nathan grins.

He sends a text to Latrice.

NATHAN

Hey, I think I have an idea to get Nadia a new assistant.

LATRICE

Really? What is it?

NATHAN

I have someone in mind, but I want to run the idea by her first. Do you know how much Nadia is paying?

LATRICE

It's 50k a year and full benefits.

NATHAN

Damn that's more than I make ☹

LATRICE

LOL!! Wow, I really am your suga-momma.

NATHAN

In that case, can I have a new car? Kind of done with the Camry.

LATRICE

Sure, just do that happy dance you promised to show me in your draws.

NATHAN

Again, I will be naked if you like.

LATRICE

I like. Are you free Friday for dinner?

NATHAN

Can we make it tomorrow?

LATRICE

Sure.

NATHAN

Great! I need to see you.

LATRICE

And I, you. Cork and Marble at seven.
I figured we could go back since we
never got to eat ☺.

NATHAN

Sounds good.

Nathan definitely needs to talk to Latrice about what happened today, and face-to-face would be better. He needs time to think of what they're going to do now that the number of people who know about them seems to be growing.

LATRICE

I'll make sure to wear something you'll
enjoy peeling off me.

And just like that, Nathan's dick is hard.

"Why are you smiling so much?" Greg breaks Nathan's concentration.

"Oh, shit. Sorry, man. I forgot you were here."

"Gee, thanks."

Amy brings them another round of beers. Nathan sips his sheepishly.

"Sorry," Nathan says after Amy leaves.

"Who were you talking to?"

Nathan sips his beer and shrugs. "Just someone I know."

"C'mon, man, tell me about her *or him*?"

"It's a her." Nathan chuckles.

"Alright then, out with it."

Nathan knows he should keep his mouth shut, but aside from the occasional text exchange with Ronnie, he has no one to talk to about this. Greg has been at Glen Oak for a while. Maybe he could give Nathan some insight into how he should navigate his relationship with a parent.

Nathan lowers his voice. "Have you ever hooked up with a parent?"

"Who told you?" Greg rolls his eyes. "It was Katie, wasn't it?"

"I have no idea what the fuck you're talking about, dude," Nathan deadpans.

"Oh." Greg blushes and drinks his beer.

"Care to share with the class, Mr. Lucas?" Nathan smirks.

"Dana Kopel," Greg mumbles.

"What?" Nathan shouts.

"Shhh!" Greg frowns.

"Sorry. I was just...Jesus Christ, man. Why?"

"As nosy as she is, that's how good she is in bed."

"You're kidding."

Greg shakes his head. Amy brings them their burgers.

Nathan grabs the ketchup and puts some on his fries. "How did that even happen?"

"Parent-teacher night. I ran into her in the hallway, and she was flirting. I was fresh from my divorce and was feeling lonely and vulnerable."

"And she pounced?"

"Like a cat on a helpless mouse." Greg bites his burger, then wipes his mouth. "I didn't stand a chance."

"*Yeesh*. How did you get out?"

"I found out about the two firings that took place in our district."

"The what now?" Nathan pauses with a fry halfway to his mouth.

"Oh, yeah. You probably haven't heard. You see, the official rule says that there's no fraternizing between parents and teachers *on campus*. It's a fireable offense. But according to everyone who knows what happened, those two teachers got fired simply for dating parents."

"Shit." Nathan's devastated.

Nathan wonders if this is why Mark confronted him today. He'll definitely try to get Nathan fired.

"How long has it been going on?" Greg sips his beer.

"Since the beginning of the school year."

"I don't suppose you want to tell me who it is."

Nathan rubs the back of his neck. "I don't know."

"I told you mine, and besides, I can keep my mouth shut, I promise. I have your back."

Nathan sighs. "Latrice Richardson. That's what had Quincy's dad was up my ass today. And I have no idea how he found out, either."

Greg's eyes light up. "Holy shit, dude. You have to find out how he knows. This could fuck things up for you big-time."

"I know." Nathan looks defeated, like he's already lost his job.

"Look, I'm just going to say this and be done. If she's worth the risk, then be careful."

Nathan nods.

They eat in silence as he considers his options. Either lose Latrice or lose his job. Neither option is one he likes.

Twenty-One

LATRICE

Latrice gives herself a quick once-over before heading to the restaurant. She picked out a backless, sleeveless burgundy dress with a deep V-neck. Her lips match her dress, and her natural hair is styled in a cascade of waves. She slips on a black coat and ties it together, smiling at herself in the mirror, knowing she's going to make Nathan drool. This dinner will be their first time really going out, and it's happening after they told each other "I love you." They're starting to feel like a real couple. She almost slipped up and blew him a kiss this morning when she dropped off Quincy. The only thing that stopped her—aside from it not being the appropriate time or place—was the look on Nathan's face when he saw her. He seemed aloof. Hopefully, whatever is bothering him will be fine by the time she meets him.

Latrice reminds herself to stop at the store tomorrow

and buy some frozen chicken wings to make as a thank-you to Thad and Nay Nay. Thad picked up Quincy from school. He and Nay Nay are taking him to the movies, then he's spending the night at Thad's place. He'll drop Quincy off at school in the morning.

Latrice's phone buzzes. It's Nathan.

NATHAN

Hey Lala. I'm so sorry but a family emergency came up and I can't meet you tonight but I do want to talk with you. Raincheck?

Raincheck? Seriously? Latrice thinks.

Latrice hates to sound selfish, but if his mother has brown water again, then she'll just need to call a plumber. Hell, Latrice will even pay for it. She has waited for too long to get Nathan alone, and she is not about to waste it. She grabs her purse and her keys and heads out the door. Nathan's apartment is about forty minutes from her and almost an hour from the school, so there's no chance of anyone seeing her. He mentioned it was a brick building by a Dunkin' Donuts on Crest Blvd. She finds parking on the street. Seeing a delivery guy at the intercom, she hurries so she can get inside behind him. She sees him press the apartment number for Woodson.

What kind of family emergency involves greasy take out? He could be having Cork & Marble followed by devouring her and this is what he chooses?

"Yes," she hears Nathan respond.

"I have your food," the delivery guy says.

"Come on up." Nathan buzzes him in.

The delivery guy opens the door, but before he can get over the threshold, Latrice taps his shoulder.

"I'll give you a nice tip if you let me take it up." She hands him a hundred.

He smiles. "Thanks, lady. It's apartment 4E."

"Thank you," Latrice says.

She takes the elevator to the fourth floor and practically stomps in her stilettos to Nathan's door. When she gets there, she knocks hard enough to wake the dead.

～

NATHAN

An hour ago, Nathan was getting ready to meet Latrice for dinner and wondering how to tell her about him possibly losing his job. *Oh!* And her ex-husband knows about them too.

Ever since drinking with Greg, he's been trying to think of how to approach things with Latrice. Agreeing to be discreet when Quincy was their biggest concern was one thing. Now that he knows he can be fired, he's scared shitless.

Nathan had been going over what to say when he heard a knock on his door. He'd looked through the peephole surprised to see Leon. Although his older brother was standing there, he wasn't the self-assured man he usually was. He was haggard and looked like he had been crying.

Nathan's heart had immediately raced. Had something happened to Momma? He'd spoken to her this morning.

Nathan opened the door in a panic. "Leon, what's going on? Is it Momma? Is she okay?"

"Momma's fine, Nate."

"So what's going on?"

"I-um. Look, Nate, I know we're not close, and I know that I fucked up any sort of real relationship between us, but…"

Tears had streamed down Leon's face. Nathan had pulled him into his arms, letting his brother weep.

"It's okay," Nathan had whispered. "It's okay, man. Let it out. Tell me what's going on when you're ready."

Leon had let go and took deep breaths. "It's Amber. We've been having all these problems. All we do lately is fight. She thinks I work too much and don't spend enough time at home. I think she's going to leave me. I don't have any real friends, Nate. Here I am riding you about your life and mine is falling apart."

"I'm sorry, Leon."

"You're in a suit. Were you going somewhere?"

"Yeah. I was, but don't worry about that. I'll cancel my plans, and you and I can talk."

"Are you sure?"

"Yeah. It'll be fine. She'll understand."

At least that was what Nathan thought.

When he opens his door for the food he ordered, he finds an incredibly sexy, gorgeous and angry Latrice instead of the delivery person.

She shoves the food into his arms. "Where the fuck do you get off canceling on me at the last minute?"

Nathan looks at Latrice wide eyed with a mix of fear, shock and horniness.

"Lala, you look amazing," Nathan manages.

"Yeah, I know."

She takes off her black coat, dropping it to the floor, and crosses her arms.

Holy fucking shit! For a split-second, Nathan considers kicking his brother out.

"I got dressed up, did my hair and got Thad and Nay Nay to watch Quincy, only for you to cancel on me."

"I'm so sorry, sweetheart, but..." Nathan opens the door further so she can see Leon. "I have a family issue. Latrice, this is my brother Leon."

"Oh." Latrice looks embarrassed. "Sorry."

She picks up her coat and puts it back on.

"Hi." Leon waves.

"Hi." Latrice smiles shyly.

"Um, I'll just be going." Latrice turns to leave.

"No. You might be able to help. Come on in. Have some food," Nathan suggests.

Latrice comes in and looks around Nathan's place. He doesn't have much in the way of furniture, but his place is simple and nice.

"Have a seat." Nathan gestures for her to sit on the couch.

He goes to work making plates for the three of them. Luckily, he ordered enough food for an army, so there's plenty to go around. He hears Latrice and Leon chatting.

"So you're the mom Nate's been dating?"

"That's me. I heard you had a lot to say about it."

"Yeah, I'm sorry about that. I should have minded my own business. Especially considering that it was Nathan's conviction about loving you that got my wife to finally confront me."

Nathan brings their plates to the coffee table and takes a seat on the couch next to Latrice.

"About what?" she asks.

"About how I need to give more time to our marriage. It just seems like whether it's our mother or now my wife, Nate can do no wrong, and I'm always trying to catch up."

"That's not true and you know it, Lee. Look, man, I love you, and I want us to be brothers. Real brothers, but you have to start showing me respect and stop pitting us against each other in your head. Momma loves us both. I just got more attention because I came into our family so late."

"I know, Nate. I just... I had a tough time—have a tough time—getting past how much things changed, and how quickly, when you arrived. One minute, Momma's talking about getting another foster kid. The next thing I knew, you were there. I never really got time to adjust."

Nathan nods his understanding. *That makes sense.* The time in between Nathan leaving the Samuels' and being placed with Momma was only two weeks. His head was spinning from the new change even after bouncing around so long; he could only imagine how Leon felt.

He feels Latrice rest her head on his shoulder and give his hand a squeeze. He loves these little gestures—it helps calm him and make him more relaxed.

Leon lets out a breath. "Nathan, you're the kid she depends on. You're the one who is always there for her. The shit with her having brown water. I tried to get that taken care of, but I became so busy with work that I forgot to call a plumber. She keeps giving me chances to show up for her, and I keep failing. Meanwhile, you never do. It's not easy to see you always being the hero."

"I'm not trying to be a hero. I just want to be there for her like she's always been there for us."

"Me too. And, I'd also like for us to open up more and be friends. Neither of us have that many." Leon places a hand on Nathan's shoulder.

"Speaking of which, how are the teacher playdates going?" Latrice asks.

"They're going well. I had beers with Greg Lucas." Nathan smirks at her.

"Is that someone he just made up? Or is that a real person?" Leon whispers loudly to Latrice.

"Nigga, I'm sitting right here." Nathan laughs.

"He's a real person." Latrice laughs too.

Nathan goes to the fridge and brings them each back a bottle of Dank Monkey.

"Dank Monkey?" Latrice looks at him like he's nuts.

"It's a goofy name, but a damn good beer." He looks at Leon. "My imaginary friend Greg turned me on to it."

"I was just fucking with you," Leon teases.

"Anyway, we're supposed to be talking about you and Amber. I think you should tell Latrice about it. I think she could help. It wouldn't hurt to get a woman's perspective."

Leon turns to Latrice. "Okay. Basically my wife Amber and I have been fighting a lot. She wants me to spend more time at home, but I'm the CEO of Chomp, a huge food delivery app. I can't just take time off."

"Boy, bye. You can easily retire at this point and spend the rest of your life spoiling your wife." Latrice playfully rolls her eyes waving Leon off.

"Yeah, but I'm a workaholic. I love what I do."

"Do you love her more?" She asks.

"Of course."

"Then cut your hours and fix your marriage. End of discussion." Latrice smirks.

She smiles and takes a sip of her beer after passing down her edict.

"Yes, ma'am."

Leon looks at Nathan, who smiles at how much of a badass his girl is. He kisses Latrice on her dimple.

"Now, why exactly does your brother have student

loan debt when you're a freaking millionaire?" Latrice asks.

"Because I offered to pay it, but he wouldn't let me."

Latrice smacks Nathan's shoulder.

"Ow!"

"What's wrong with you? Take his money."

"Okay, damn. You supposed to be handling him."

"I can multitask."

"Now, on to you two kids. Isn't dating Latrice a conflict of interest or something?" Leon asks.

"Not really, but we're being discreet," Latrice answers.

"Actually." Nathan begins.

"What is it?" Latrice asks.

He really didn't want to tell her like this, but here goes.

"I found out from Greg that some teachers who used to work in our district and dated parents were fired. And your ex-husband knows."

"What? Are you serious?" Latrice stares at him in shock. "How?"

"I have no idea. I've been racking my brain trying to figure out how he could possibly have found out."

"Oh, my God," Latrice says softly.

The look of devastation on her face rips Nathan apart. In that moment, he knows what he has to do.

"I don't care that he knows, and if I get fired, I'll figure things out. All I know is that I'm not giving you up." Nathan takes her face in his hand.

"But Nathan—"

"No. What did you just tell Leon? You mean more to me than my job, Latrice."

"Look, y'all, I've only been around you for half an hour and I can tell that you're a good match for each other. I can make some calls and help Nate get a teaching job anywhere," Leon offers.

"But he really loves working at Glen Oak." Latrice squeezes Nathan's hand.

"Then it sounds like you two need to figure something out." Leon smiles.

The three of them talk, laugh and eat more. Hours pass and Leon makes his leave. Nathan walks him to the door.

"Thanks for putting up with me tonight, Nate."

"Nothing further from the truth, man. I got you."

The brothers hug.

"Don't let her go. She's a keeper," Leon says.

"So is Amber."

"True. I'll see you."

"Aight."

Nathan closes the door and faces Latrice.

"I should get going too," Latrice teases.

Nathan shakes his head. "Nope. I'm taking your fine ass into my bedroom, and I'm peeling that dress off you —like you asked—then I'm going to lick every inch of your body, and you're going to stay the night."

"Is that so, Mr. Woodson?"

"That is so."

Nathan picks Latrice up and throws her over his shoulder.

"Ahh! Nathan." Latrice laughs.

Nathan smacks her ass and smiles as Latrice's laughter fills the room.

Nathan's bare hands gripped tightly as he held his own hands.

At that Latrice laughed.

Nathan made breakfast and smiled as Latrice laughed at all the jokes.

Twenty-Two
LATRICE

It's winter break and Latrice and Drea are at the office doing some last-minute inventory and data entry before they close the boutique for two weeks. Latrice got to the bottom of Mark's knowledge of her and Nathan. It turns out that the day before Mark confronted Nathan, he and Drea had dinner with their parents. When Drea went to the ladies' room and left her phone at the table, Mark picked it up when he saw Latrice's name and read the text. Nadia sent Drea a silly text about Latrice and Nathan. Drea got this info out of Mark by threatening to hit him again. He spilled the beans immediately. At which point Drea punched him on his arm anyway.

Mark has been traveling overseas for work so Latrice hasn't had a chance to speak with him. And he didn't bring it up when she spoke to him yesterday to finalize holiday plans. She is scheduled to drop off Quincy at

Mark's on Christmas Eve. The compromise for Quincy not spending half of the winter break with Mark was for him to spend all of Christmas Eve with him. Latrice plans on having a talk with Mark then.

"How have things been for you and Nathan?" Drea asks as she sorts through some skirts.

"Tortuous." Latrice sighs.

"Why?"

"Because ever since we found out he could get fired, we've decided to cool off on seeing each other. We're going to try and start things up again once I talk to Mark and once Dana is off our tail."

"I thought Rachel put her in her place."

"She did, but Dana is proving to be a dog with a bone about this. She told some folks about Mark confronting Nathan, and speculation is running wild among her coven. Thankfully, no one else seems to care, but if that changes, I may have to ask Rachel to pull the trigger on her threat."

"Sounds like you should."

"I saw her and the other clucking hens talking and pointing at me during a PTA meeting a couple of days ago."

"Those women really don't have anything better to do with their time?"

"Of course not. They're bored housewives. This is entertainment for them."

Drea nods.

"Any thought to what you're going to say to my idiot brother?"

That's all Latrice has thought about—and Nathan, of course—for the past month. Mark has a lot of fucking nerve demanding that Nathan stop seeing her. Especially after everything he put her through.

"I have my speech for Mark locked and loaded."

"Good. Oh, Mom wanted me to tell you hi. You know she still holds out hope that you and Mark will get back together."

"*Shiiittt*. Not in this lifetime, but enough about me. How did your date with the NASCAR guy go?"

"Ugh!" Drea rolls her eyes.

"That bad?"

"Worse. The guy was a complete moron. I asked him what was the last book he read, and he looked at me like he didn't know what a book was."

Latrice burst out laughing. She clutches a nearby table to keep from falling over.

"I pictured him doing that thing that dogs do when they tilt their heads and look confused." Latrice cackles.

"Girl, that's pretty much what he did." Drea cracks up.

"Don't worry, sis. You'll find the one someday." Latrice squeezes her shoulders.

"I hope so. Maybe I should have Nay Nay take me to Cork & Marble so I can find a one-night stand. Hell, it worked wonders for you."

"That's a possibility."

Latrice has hinted at Drea giving Thad a shot, but Drea made it clear that he was a no-go. Latrice still thinks her reasoning is hogwash, but she won't press the issue.

On Christmas Eve morning, Latrice and Quincy arrive at Mark's house.

She knocks on the door, and Mark answers it, wearing a holiday sweater and dark jeans. Quincy told Latrice that Mark insisted everyone wear holiday sweaters for a family photo by the tree.

"Quincy, why don't you go in the kitchen with Acacia and the twins? Chef Nikolas is making a chocolate fountain." Mark smiles.

"Cool." Quincy runs off into the house.

"We need to talk," Mark says. There's a definite bite in his tone Latrice does not appreciate.

He gestures for her to join him in the gazebo in the backyard. Latrice takes a seat.

"Yes," Latrice says in a mockingly innocent tone.

"Don't be flippant, Latrice. You know what this is about. You're fucking Quincy's teacher."

"Yeah, so?"

"So? You don't see how inappropriate that is?"

"Are you serious, Mark?"

"Look, I'm not proud of how I treated our marriage, but I never fucked around with anyone who had a direct tie to our son."

"You fucked his nanny, fool," Latrice says flatly.

"Oh, shit. That's right." Mark says. "Whatever, the point is—"

"The point is this isn't any of your business. What goes on between me and Nathan is between the two of us."

"Not if it affects Quincy."

"And it hasn't. Quincy doesn't even know. Nathan and I will tell him at the end of the school year when he is no longer his teacher."

"Just tell him now. Quincy's a smart kid. And if he likes the guy, it shouldn't be a problem, right?"

God. I hate it when he gets all smug like this.

"It's complicated." She folds her arms across her chest.

"What could possibly...? Oh my God. You guys aren't supposed to be seeing each other, are you? He could get fired, couldn't he?" Mark grins.

Latrice rolls her eyes as he laughs.

"Oh, this is too good. Maybe I should call Principal Tanaka."

"Stop it, Mark!" Latrice barks.

He smirks, getting close to Latrice and looking her in the eyes.

"Why? This is unbelievable. All your grandstanding about what's best for Quincy and you're dating his teacher, and the poor SOB is putting his *low-paying* job in jeopardy over some pussy."

Latrice slaps Mark. He went way too far. He looks at her with venom in his eyes. She has tears in hers.

"You are such an asshole. You put me through hell. I loved you, wholly and completely, and you broke my heart. When I found you with Acacia, you were on top of her, moaning her name, and she looked right at me and smiled," Latrice says. Her anger is palpable.

Mark's anger melts and is replaced with shame. He looks away from her.

She continues, "And now I found someone who cares for me way more than you ever did. So much so that he's willing to lose his job, one that he loves, to be with me. You never loved me that much if you ever loved me at all."

"Of course I loved you. Hell, I still do." Mark looks at her, speaking with conviction.

"Oh, fuck off," Latrice spits, turning her back to him.

"Latrice, please."

When she turns around, Mark has a look of deep sincerity in his eyes. Latrice is thrown—she's never seen him look that vulnerable before.

"I mean it. I am a fool. I thought that our marriage would be like my parents. I'd go out and play, and you would stay. But I should have known better. You were strong. You are strong, and you would never let any man belittle you. And I tried at every turn. Especially with your business. I thought that if I made you small, made you need me, then you wouldn't leave. I fucked up big-time. But please know that it was never because I didn't love you. Because I do. And I always have."

There's a silence between the two. Latrice wipes her eyes and releases a deep breath. She can't believe what she's hearing.

"I'm sorry, what?"

"Look, if Nathan does get fired, it won't be because of me," Mark says.

He walks back into the house. Latrice runs her fingers through her hair and closes her eyes. When the fuck did her life become such a soap opera?

Nathan plays in the backyard with his niece and nephew. Even though he and Latrice aren't seeing each other until the coast is clear, he sent her a picture of himself making a silly face while wearing one of the holiday sweaters Amber made for everyone. She and Leon are hosting Christmas this year.

His phone buzzes. He smiles, knowing it's her reply.

Nathan takes out his phone. "I'll be right back, kids."

"Okay, Uncle Nate." Tyler smiles.

The kids continue to laugh as they come back inside and help Leon put more ornaments on the tree. Nathan passes by Amber as she carries a tray of cookies to bring to them. He snatches one, and she smacks his hand playfully. He smiles at her while taking a bite. She rolls her eyes.

"Kids, cookies!" she announces.

They stop what they're doing for a cookie break.

Nathan heads to a guest room and closes the door before reading Latrice's text.

LATRICE

Mark's doing the same thing!! Has Quincy, the twins and Acacia wearing those corny ass sweaters for holiday pictures.

NATHAN

I'm sure Q's real happy about that.

LATRICE

LOL. He's enduring.

NATHAN

Did you and Mark talk?

LATRICE

Yeah, it was weirdly emotional.

NATHAN

How so?

LATRICE

He admitted that he still loves me.

What? Nathan frowns at his phone as he rereads Latrice's words. He can't be too surprised. Mark was weirdly protective when he confronted him. Nathan thought it was because of Quincy, but it makes sense he would still feel something for Latrice. She's an amazing woman.

NATHAN

How did you take it?

LATRICE

Didn't say anything for a while. I was pretty shocked but he did say he wouldn't say anything to get you fired.

NATHAN

That's good. How did you manage that? I was sure he was ready to rat me out.

Nathan was so sure that he took Leon up on his offer to look into which schools were hiring. Unfortunately, Leon's contacts reported there's been a hiring freeze across many school districts due to budget constraints. Even private, charter and magnet schools are feeling the crunch.

LATRICE

I slapped him.

Nathan calls her. She answers after the second ring.

"You did what?" Nathan asks.

"You read that right. He was being disrespectful and smug, so I slapped him and confessed how his treatment of our marriage affected me. He was remorseful. That's when he told me he still loved me and said he wouldn't say anything."

"Wow. Go, Lala! Look at you. Your fine ass has two men after you."

"Yeah, but I only want one of them."

Latrice's voice is sultry and low. It makes his dick ready to go. He has to stand and adjust himself.

"It's me, right?" Nathan jokes.

"Shut up." Latrice laughs.

"I miss you," he confesses. "I know it hasn't been that long since we've seen each other, but I needed to tell you that."

"I miss you too."

"Latrice! Where did you go?" Nadia yells in the background.

"I'm in here. Keep your voice down. I'm talking to Nathan."

Nathan can hear them arguing as Nadia attempts to take the phone from Latrice.

"Hey, Nate Dawg!" Nadia won the phone battle.

"Hi, Nadia. How are you? Merry Christmas." Nathan chuckles.

"Merry Christmas. I'm good. What you up to?"

"Chilling with my family."

"What are y'all doing in here? I'm the only one helping Mom," Nathan hears Thad call out to Nadia and Latrice.

"We're talking to Nathan," Nadia says.

"Correction. I was talking to Nathan—you butted in," Latrice corrects her sister.

"Thad, stop it," Nadia says.

"Quiet, little woman," Thad says. And now he's on the phone. "What's up, man?"

"What's up, Thad? How you doin', bruh?"

"I got a bone to pick with you, homey."

Nathan laughs. He should have suspected some over-protective brother energy from such a big-ass dude.

"What did I do?" Nathan asks.

"Thanks to you, *Mister Woodson*, Q's talking about becoming a teacher. He's supposed to take over my barbershops. He said some shit about how cool it's been having a Black man as his teacher or some shit," Thad playfully mocks.

Nathan bursts out laughing. He's touched. Quincy's such a great kid, and it's been a joy teaching and getting to know him.

"Look, Q is a smart little man. I'm sure he'll figure out a way to do both," Nathan replies.

Thad lets out a hearty laugh. "You right."

"What is going on in here?"

Nathan hears an older woman with a slight accent. She must be Latrice's mother. Nathan gets nervous at the prospect of speaking with her.

"We're talking to Tricey's boyfriend," Thad admits.

"Damn momma's boy," Nathan hears Latrice grumble. This makes him smirk. His smile fades as there's now an ominous silence.

"Hello, young man. I'm Janet, Latrice's mother."

"Hello, Mrs. Richardson," Nathan chokes out.

He clears his throat, hoping to shake the nervous energy out of his voice.

"You sound nervous. No reason for that. I can't grab you over the phone, can I?"

"I don't know. From what Latrice has told me, you might be able to."

Janet laughs. "My daughter Nadia is the one with a flair for the dramatic, but Latrice has her moments as well."

"That she does." There's a small bit of silence between them. Nathan decides to fill it by laying his cards on the table. "Mrs. Richardson, I know you had concerns about my relationship with Latrice and how it will affect Quincy. I want to assure you that his well-being is of the utmost importance to me and Latrice. As soon as we figure out a way to navigate our relationship without me losing my job, we plan on telling him."

"I know, young man. And I appreciate your candor. Latrice made it clear to me that what you two share is bigger than a casual relationship. She truly does love you."

A warm surge goes through Nathan's body at hearing those words. He already knows that Latrice loves him, but hearing it from someone so close to her makes him feel like he can conquer the world.

"Goodbye, Nathan. You be sure to come by for dinner soon."

"I will. Thank you. Goodbye, Mrs. Richardson."

"I'll let you get back to your family before my dad wants to talk to you." Latrice gets back on the phone.

"Right. They're probably wondering where the hell I went." He chuckles.

"I'll call you later tonight."

"I look forward to it."

They hang up, and Nathan soaks in their conversation. He smiles, then gets up to rejoin everyone.

He sees them all sitting around the table waiting for him. The table is covered with food. Turkey, dressing, a ham, a roast, mashed potatoes, mac and cheese, greens, rolls and yams.

"It's about time, man. We were about to start eating without you," Leon jokes.

"Sorry, y'all. Had an important call I had to take."

"And how is Latrice?" Amber asks.

"She's good." Nathan blushes.

"More importantly, when am I going to meet her?" Momma Ernie insists.

"You will, Momma. I promise."

Nathan takes a seat, and they all pass around the food and pile their plates. Not once does Leon bring up old times, and not once does Nathan check the time to see if four hours have passed.

Twenty-Four

NATHAN.

"Welcome back from your holiday break, and happy New Year! We have a lot of fun activities coming up at Glen Oak from now until the end of the school year. We have the Valentine's Day Jamboree happening next month and Field Day happening in March. And please remember that next Monday there's no school in observation of Dr. King's birthday. And finally, standardized testing is right around the corner." Principal Tanaka makes her morning announcements through the PA system. The kids groan at the last announcement.

"Alright, y'all, cool it." Nathan smiles at their dramatics.

"Glen Oak hopes to receive more funding this year, so we're all going to need to buckle down and get those test scores higher than last year's" Principal Tanaka continues. "I know we can do it, Mustangs. Lunch today is your choice of chicken nuggets, corn dogs or grilled cheese. Let's make it a good day!"

"Okay, first assignment of the new year. We're going to switch things up again and have English first. I want you to partner up, and we're going to make collages of our favorite books."

This schedule is for the next few days. This morning, Nathan learned a student from Woodcrest Middle School would come to work with Ashleigh B., but their tutoring elective is in the afternoon. So Nathan switched English with math so the tutor could be in the classroom and see the lesson in real time to better help Ashleigh. Nathan has requested a student with a morning elective, but like most things in education, the student placement is moving at a glacial pace.

He overhears Ashleigh and Quincy talking.

"Quincy, do you want to be my partner? I mean, if you're already Eli's, then—"

"No, he's partnering up with Charlie. I can be your partner."

"Cool. I have some ideas for books we can use."

"Me too."

They start talking about the books they want to use and agree quickly on *The Boxcar Children*. Ashleigh pulls out her book, and they go through it looking for objects to include in their collage.

Nathan grins to himself. Seeing Ashleigh come out

of her shell and become friends with Quincy has been so rewarding. He considered asking Leon for a job at Chomp so he and Latrice could finally tell Quincy, but seeing things like this—the little victories that come with this job—makes him rethink his decision yet again. To her credit, Latrice has been more than patient with him as he's gone back and forth. He suspects it's because she's a little nervous about telling Quincy herself.

Nathan sits at his desk. School has just ended, and he's grading the day's assignments.

"Mr. Woodson."

He looks up and sees Lauren Bennett in the doorway looking slightly apprehensive.

"I hope I'm not disturbing you," she says.

"No, not at all. Come on in."

Nathan is pleased to see her. He's been trying to talk with her after school but she's always in a rush.

"I wanted to thank you for all your help with Ashleigh. Getting her a tutor and the whole mess with the bullies."

"It's my pleasure."

Ms. Bennett turns to leave. "I'll be out of your way. Ashleigh's waiting in the car with my auntie. I have to take them both home. My auntie is helping with Ashleigh now that her dad has been working double shifts."

"Actually, Mrs. Bennett," Nathan calls out. She turns to face him, "I wanted to talk to you about you and your husband's work situation, if I may."

"Okay."

"I understand that you and your husband feel that the both of you working so hard is necessary to help Ashleigh's development, but I think I may have found a way for you to only work one job."

"Really? How?"

"I found out that Latrice Richardson's sister runs a law firm and she's looking for a new assistant. The pay would be more than enough, and the firm isn't that far from the school."

"Oh my God! That would be amazing."

Nathan takes out his phone. "I'll text you the information."

Nathan exchanges info with Mrs. Bennett.

"Give Nadia a call."

"I will. Thank you again. I'll have to thank Latrice too. Bye, Mr. Woodson."

"Bye, Mrs. Bennett."

Later as Nathan walks to his car, he pulls out his phone, calling Latrice.

"Hey!" she says. Her voice sounds upbeat and cheerful.

God, he loves how excited she sounds whenever he calls her. It makes him love her even more.

"Hey. I gave Nadia's info to the potential new assistant."

"Great. Do you want to tell me who it is now?"

"Lauren Bennett."

"Awesome, she's so sweet. I'm sure she'll be a huge

help to Nay Nay. I'll talk her up too. Hopefully, she gets the job."

"Mrs. Bennett was really appreciative. She wants to thank you as well."

"I can invite her to lunch. It'll be a good opportunity for me and Rach to get to know Lauren too. I see her after school all the time, and she never really interacts with the other moms. I should make more of an effort to talk to her."

Nathan loves how giving and selfless Latrice is. She's always ready to help people, no matter what.

"I'm going to marry you and put a baby in you." He grins.

"Is that your idea of a proposal?" Latrice laughs.

"I'm just letting you know. I'm going to spend the rest of my life showing you how much I love you."

"Quincy's at Rachel's house. I can text her and ask if he can stay over. You want me to stop by your place and you can show me how much you love me all night?"

"Why you asking questions you already know the answer to?"

Latrice's laughter fills Nathan's ear and makes him wish she was in his arms right that minute. He gets in his car and heads toward his apartment.

"I'm on my way home now."

"That gives me some time. I think I'll make you some wings."

"Lemon pepper?" Nathan's voice is filled with hope.

"Yes, baby. Lemon pepper. Anything for my man."

"Woman, I'm about to make your toes curl."

"Looking forward to it. I'll see you in a bit."

"See you, my love."

Twenty-Five

LATRICE

Three months later, Latrice, Drea, Nadia and Rachel are at Trader Joe's looking for stuff to bring to Dana's annual Spring Break bonfire. Latrice isn't happy to be going, but Nathan's going to be there and thanks to life, lifing they haven't had much time to be together since January. Aside from the usual stuff like work—she's been traveling back and forth to New York for business--and trying to be careful thanks to Dana and her annoying ass coven, there have been more worthwhile reasons why they've been apart. Namely Nathan and Leon have been spending more time together. Both are making an effort to strengthen their brotherly bond and while Latrice could not be more happy for them, the lack of Nathan in her life has left her feeling antsy. This is the most time they have spent apart since they met. They still talk on the phone but the last time she physically saw him was during parent/teacher night last month. And she couldn't exactly bone him then. That would have defeated the whole purpose of them sneaking around. Hell, she obviously can't do anything with him at the bonfire either but at least she'll get to see him...and in swim trunks.

She's definitely been feeling an ache in her heart from this involuntary break, not to mention her pussy, which has basically become sentient and throbs at the very thought of Nathan. Her damn cootie cat is not happy and wants to know when she can play with Nathan's dick again. It doesn't help that they live so far from each other. The new changes in their schedule have made going to his place for sneaky links damn near impossible.

"This is fucking ridiculous. Who the hell gives food assignments for a bonfire? You just get ingredients for s'mores and call it a day," Nadia says.

"Dana. That's who." Latrice sighs.

"I still think you should let Rachel destroy her." Drea says.

Latrice decided not to let Rachel go through with her threat. She came to the conclusion that it would only attract more attention making it even harder for her and Nathan to see each other. Not to mention Dana successfully outwitted them by announcing that Brad's Fourth of July pool party would be taking place at a palatial estate in Calabasas courtesy of her ex-husband. And while Rachel is well-liked and popular, no amount of shit talking on her part would stop anyone from attending that party. It's no secret how much Dana and her ex hate each other, so Latrice can only imagine what Dana had to do to make that happen.

Latrice laughs then lets out a weary sigh. "No, it's not worth it. But I have to say, not being able to be a real couple is starting to wear on Nathan and I. Hell, we didn't even get to do anything on Valentine's Day. We just talked on the phone as usual."

"Are you still going to tell Quincy at the end of the year?" Drea asks.

"No, we talked yesterday and decided to sit Quincy down and tell him after the bonfire. We don't want to keep this from him any longer. Besides, school ends in two months and him knowing will be one less thing we have to worry about." Latrice answers.

"That makes sense. No point in putting it off anymore with summer right around the corner." Drea replies.

"And if, by some chance, the school finds out, Nathan's prepared to resign." Latrice lets out her breath.

She can't help but be heartbroken. Nathan keeps telling her it isn't her fault. But she feels guilty he's chosen to leave Glen Oak if it comes to that. The kids love him, and he loves working there. Between Ashleigh doing better in school and Quincy having another strong Black man in his life, it's obvious how much of an impact Nathan has made at the school during his short tenure. There's no telling how much more he could accomplish.

"It sucks that Nathan might have to leave, but him

being willing to do that tells me just how much he loves you," Drea says.

"That's true." Latrice gives her a weak smile.

"Hey, don't do that. Don't overthink it," Rachel says. "You didn't force him to do this. You both discussed it and made the decision together. And he can always work for his brother."

"You're right." Latrice tries to sound convincing, but she knows that no matter how great Chomp is, Nathan's heart won't be in it.

Two days later, Latrice, Rachel, Tim, Eli and Quincy park at Dockweiler Beach and find the rest of the guests. There are at least fifty kids and their parents in attendance. The kids are enjoying the ocean and building sandcastles while the parents chat and enjoy the food. Latrice spots Nathan.

"Hello, Mr. Woodson. It's good to see you." Latrice plays it cool, but she can't help but stare at him like he's lunch.

"You too, Ms. Richardson."

"You plan on getting in the water?"

"Why? You want a sequel to the dunk tank?"

Latrice lowers her voice. "I certainly wouldn't mind that."

"Careful, Lala," Nathan mumbles.

They eye each other for a moment. Latrice's eyes travel from Nathan's head to his toes. He has on solid black swim trunks and a matching T-shirt. Latrice's face gets hot as she soaks him in. She sees a man pushing a cart selling drinks nearby.

"I'm going to get a lemonade." She smiles, displaying her dimples.

"You know what seeing those dimples does to me," Nathan growls.

"Control yourself, Mr. Woodson."

"Stop making it *hard*, Ms. Richardson."

Rachel walks up to them. "You two need to separate pronto."

"What? Why?" Latrice asks.

"Because you're in the vicinity of children eye-fucking each other. The only reason Dana hasn't noticed is because I sent Tim over to distract her."

Latrice and Nathan look and, sure enough, Tim is channeling his inner Chris Hemsworth, grinning and flexing much to the delight of Dana and her coven.

"On the count of three, I want you two to go your separate ways," Rachel orders.

"Rachel," Nathan begins.

"Hush up. I don't want to hear it. One, two, three. Split!"

Nathan rushes away, looking slightly scared of Rachel. While Latrice is dragged over to the drink cart.

Two hours pass, and Latrice and Nathan have avoided each other successfully. Unfortunately, she is about to go mad. Seeing him in the water playing with the kids has made her so hot and bothered, she takes herself underneath the pier a few feet away to think.

Latrice closes her eyes and gives herself a pep talk.

"You can do this. It's just a few more hours. Then we'll tell Quincy, get through the rest of the school year and this will all be over."

Feeling calmer, she opens her eyes and sees Nathan heading toward her. Before she can say anything, his hands hold her face as their lips connect.

"Nathan, what are you--?"

He kisses her again before she can finish.

"I'm sorry, Lala," he utters while kissing and biting her neck.

Latrice knows she should stop him, but she can't. Her pussy has officially overridden her brain and is doing all the thinking now.

She returns his kiss and rakes her nails against his back.

"How did you get past Rachel?"

"I waited until she was distracted by Eli and made my escape."

"How did you know she'd be distracted by him?"

"I may or may not have exhausted him and some other kids by playing with them for the past hour. When I saw you walk over here, I suggested they get some food and chill before playing again. I may have bought us at least ten minutes before Rachel notices we're both gone."

"With Rach, it's more like five. Eli can't get away with shit because the woman notices everything."

"Let's stop wasting time, then."

They kiss some more. Nathan leaves a trail of kisses down Latrice's chest to her stomach.

"Do you have any idea how difficult it's been not to take you over my shoulder and rip this two-piece off you?"

Latrice smiles. She does look rather good in her orange two-piece that makes her breasts and ass look fabulous. She made sure to bring a coverall but ditched it when she got in the water earlier with Rach and some of the other moms. It was still a little wet, making her nipples very noticeable.

"No, tell me."

Instead, he shows her how much he wants her by turning her around so her back is to him while kissing and nibbling her neck. He rubs his dick up against her ass and moans.

"Fuck, Lala."

His hands cup her breasts while he kisses, licks and sucks on her neck. Latrice reaches up and rubs the back of his head. She closes her eyes and...

"Oh my God!"

Latrice and Nathan turn and see Dana standing under the pier looking at them.

"I'm sorry. I was just coming back from the ladies' room," Dana says, her voice dripping with smug satisfaction.

"Uh, we were. We, um," Nathan sputters.

"Nathan. Just don't." Latrice says, defeated.

"Well, when you two are done, we're about to make s'mores." Dana smiles, then walks away.

"How long do you think we have?" Nathan asks.

"She's texting her coven as we speak. We're toast," Latrice says. "I'm sorry, Nathan. You're going to have to resign now, and with a scandal, it's going to make it hard for you to get another teaching job."

"It's okay, Lala. Honestly, I'm kind of happy to have this off our backs."

"Me too. But..." Latrice looks away.

Nathan lifts her face up by her chin. "But, what?"

"I wish we had told Quincy sooner. Now he's going to find out from God knows who."

"It's okay, baby. We'll stick with the plan and tell him together. We'll answer any questions he has and apologize for keeping it from him. We were trying to protect him. He'll understand."

"I hope you're right."

Nathan pulls her to him and holds her tight. Latrice rests her head on his chest and prays Nathan is right.

Twenty-Six

LATRICE

Latrice paces in her living room. The ride home with Quincy was quiet. She knows he must have heard something because when she and Nathan came back to the bonfire separately, all eyes were on them. Rachel pulled her aside and confirmed they had been outed. Even though she wanted to hightail it out of there, Latrice stayed for another hour and a half to not look suspicious. Also, she didn't want to force Quincy to leave, so she spent the remaining time fielding questions from thirsty moms about Nathan's "prowess." She basically said, "No comment," and waited until she could take her son home. Once they arrived home, Latrice told Quincy to take a shower and wash his hair. She told him he needed to come back out when he finished getting dressed so they could talk. Nathan wanted to go home and change before he came by. She's hoping that by the time Quincy is done getting ready, Nathan will be here.

There's a knock on the door. Latrice opens it and sees Nathan looking as fine as can be in a pair of jeans and a solid black T-shirt with sneakers. Whenever he dresses casually, she can really see just how young he is.

"Hey, Lala." He greets her with a sweet, nervous smile.

"Hey, Nathan." She smiles back.

"Moment of truth. You ready?"

"We really don't have a choice but to be."

Nathan takes her hand and walks her over to the couch where they take a seat.

"How was he on the ride home?"

"Quiet. He just played with his phone."

"Did he seem upset?"

"Not really."

They hear Quincy's bedroom door open and straighten. Latrice chuckles at the idea of being nervous to talk to her eight -year-old. Nathan squeezes her hand.

"I feel like we're a couple of kids and I'm about to be grilled by your dad," Nathan says.

"I was just thinking the same thing." Latrice smiles up at him.

Nathan kisses her on top of her head as Quincy enters.

"Mom, did you still want to talk to me?" He notices Nathan. "Hi, Mr. Woodson."

"Yes, sweetie. Nathan and I both wanted to talk to you. Come have a seat."

Quincy sits next to them on the couch.

"Is this about what people were saying at the bonfire?" Quincy asks.

"Yes. First, tell me what you heard," Latrice replies.

"That you and Mr. Woodson were kissing and stuff."

"Well, we were kissing, but there wasn't any stuff."

There was, but he doesn't need to know that.

"The point is, Nathan and I are in love, and we wanted to check in with you and see if you had any questions for us."

"How long have you two been in love?"

"I don't know about your mom, Q, but I fell in love with her the minute I saw her."

Latrice looks at Nathan lovingly. "Me too."

She turns her attention back to Quincy.

"Are you okay with this, sweetie?"

Quincy looks at them and offers a sweet smile. "Yeah. I am."

"Really?"

"Yeah, I like Mr. Woodson. He's cool. You look really happy, Mom."

"Thanks, Q. You're cool too, man." Nathan smiles. "Does this mean I get to learn the handshake too?"

"Sure. I'll teach it to you."

"Come here, Quince." Latrice holds her arms open.

Quincy comes over to her, and she gives him a big hug.

"Thank you, baby." Latrice holds her son's face in her hands.

"You're welcome, mom. I haven't seen you this

happy, ever. And as long as you two don't fight like dad and Acacia, I'm good."

"I'm glad you're not upset, baby. Not to switch gears, but are your dad and Acacia still acting up?"

"Big-time. They got into such a huge fight last time I was over there that Acacia threw a lamp at Dad, and he was screaming. I had to take the twins to a neighbor's house. The only reason they stopped is because the neighbor threatened to call the cops."

"Quincy, why didn't you tell me?"

Quincy looks away. "Dad asked me not to."

"Is that right?" Latrice is pissed.

Latrice kisses Quincy, then grabs her purse. "Don't worry, baby. I'll go talk to your dad."

"Your dad's going to get it, isn't he?" Nathan mumbles to Quincy.

"Oh, yeah," Quincy replies.

Latrice takes out her car keys and heads to the door. She looks over her shoulder at her two boys. "Nathan, order a pizza for dinner."

"Yes, Lala." He smiles.

"Be back in a bit." Latrice smiles back as Nathan and Quincy wave.

～

She parks her car in front of Mark's house, gets out and stomps to the front door. Leave it to this motherfucker to ruin a nice moment between her, her man and their son. Latrice pounds on the door. Mark answers, and she can't believe her eyes.

Mark's eyes are bloodshot. He looks like he hasn't slept in days and is wearing silk pajamas and a matching robe. He has a glass of dark liquid in his hand.

"Mark, you look like shit," Latrice blurts out.

"Nice to see you too, Latrice." He opens the door wider to let her in.

Latrice enters, and the house is eerily quiet. "Where are the twins?"

"They're at the park with the nanny."

"Nanny? Since when do you have a nanny?"

"Since Acacia left."

"Where did she go?"

"Who the fuck knows? All I know is she left a note saying she was tired and didn't want to be tied down to me anymore. She went on to accuse me of still being in love with you..."

Which you are.

"... and she went on to say that she never wanted kids and only had the twins to keep me in line."

"Jesus," was all Latrice could say.

"I guess I brought this on myself. With all the hurt and pain I caused, it was only a matter of time before karma caught up with me. Hell, who am I kidding?

Karma has had me by the balls for years. The two worst mistakes I ever made were losing you and marrying her."

Damn. Latrice was ready to set Mark straight and discuss Quincy's visitation, but he had to go and ruin it by being all pathetic and sad.

She lets out a sigh and follows him into the living room and takes a seat.

"What are you going to do?" she asks.

"I don't know. I got the nanny, but aside from that, I don't know what my next move is. I can't even serve her divorce papers since I don't know where she is. I'm alone. I'm all alone in this. The kids deserve better. At least Quincy has you. What do the twins have? Me and a mother who doesn't want them." Mark has tears in his eyes.

Latrice takes his hand. "They have Drea, me, your parents and now Nathan. They have plenty of adults in their lives who will step up and help. You have all the folks you need to build a village for those kids. How about this? Brunch every Sunday, at my house. And the twins can stay over from time to time."

Mark smiles and nods. Latrice is happy to see him more at ease.

"We'll ease the babies and you into this new phase. Sound good?"

"Yeah, thank you. I don't know how you're going to convince Drea. She absolutely fucking hates me."

"Your sister doesn't hate you, Mark."

"I don't know if I believe that, but thank you,

Latrice. You're the best ex-wife a poor son-of-a bitch like me could ask for."

"I know." She winks.

Mark chuckles, then wipes his eyes. "For what it's worth, I am so sorry about everything. I hope Nathan realizes how lucky he is."

"He does."

"Good. I'm happy for you. I really am."

"Thank you."

Latrice reaches over and gives him a hug. Today has become a day full of surprises, and she couldn't be happier.

Twenty—Seven

NATHAN

Nathan walks down the halls of Glen Oak and feels a bittersweet feeling. Today is the day he's putting in his notice. He starts at Chomp next week in the Market/Research department. He's going to be part of a team that predicts trends in food delivery. As if he knows what the fuck that means. The only trend he knows when it comes to food delivery is, people get hungry, they order food, then they eat it. He's not ungrateful. Thanks to his new relationship with Leon, he's not dreading his new job, it's just not where he wants to be.

Nathan stands outside Principal Tanaka's office. He's almost relieved he won't have to go into detail about why he's leaving. Surely Principal Tanaka knows about him and Latrice. He hopes the work he has put in over his eight months working there keeps going with whoever replaces him. Lauren Bennett has contacted him more than once. Ashleigh's been participating more in class and is doing much better in math. Not only that, but Nadia hired Lauren and even gave her an advance so she could quit both of her jobs immediately. Ms. Bennett thanked Nathan profusely for everything. Tears form in his eyes. He's going to miss being here. He's going to miss the kids. He's going to miss making a difference in their lives. This hurts, but being with the woman he loves is more than worth it.

Nathan knocks on Principal Tanaka's office door.

"Come in," she calls out.

Nathan enters, and she looks up and smiles.

"Good morning, Mr. Woodson."

"Good morning, Principal Tanaka."

"Have a seat. How can I help you?"

Nathan sits. "I'm just going to come out and say that my time here at Glen Oak has been tremendous. I have enjoyed every minute of working here, and I wanted to thank you for the opportunity."

Principal Tanaka looks alarmed. "Nathan, why do you sound like you're quitting?"

"Because I am. I'm giving my notice."

"Why?" Principal Tanaka stands from her seat, looking dumbstruck.

"I'm aware of the unofficial policy for fraternization between parents and teachers. I entered into a personal relationship with Latrice Richardson, as I'm sure you know—"

"I heard some things, but I thought it was just gossiping moms," Principal Tanaka interjects.

"It's not. We've been seeing each other since the beginning of the school year. I'm sorry, Erin, but I can't end things with her. I love her. So I have made the difficult decision to move on. I hope you understand."

Principal Tanaka takes her seat. "You've been talking to some of the teachers, haven't you?"

"Yes. Well, one of them."

"Nathan," Principal Tanaka shakes her head and chuckles, "There isn't a no zero-tolerance policy for parents and teachers. Unofficial or otherwise. It's just like your employee handbook says: no fraternization on school grounds."

"Really?"

"Yes, really. I mean, c'mon, how would I even enforce that? By following you and Latrice everywhere you go? As long as you haven't done anything inappropriate on campus, you're good."

Nathan has no idea what to say. He and Latrice have been tripping all over themselves so Quincy would be okay and he wouldn't get fired, and neither of those things was even a concern.

"Allow me to explain." Principal Tanaka closes her office door. "What I'm about to tell you cannot leave this room, Mr. Woodson."

"Of course."

"There were two teachers at two different schools that happen to be a part of our district, who were terminated. The reason they were terminated was never disclosed because the district paid a PR firm to keep it quiet. The discourse every school in the district would have had to endure from parents and the media would have been insane."

Nathan listens intently.

"These two teachers were dating parents, but they also chose to make videos together and with said parents for Only Fans on school grounds. That's why they were fired. Subsequently, both parents also quietly took their kids out of each school. Like I said, the district kept it close to the chest. The only thing most faculty and staff knew was that the teachers were in relationships with parents. I can only guess the amount of speculation this caused."

Nathan, still unable to speak, just looks at her.

She continues, "In hindsight, I probably should reiterate what the actual policy is to stop all this confusion."

"So I'm not in danger of losing my job?" Nathan says finally.

"Hell no! Nathan, you joining the Glen Oak faculty has been one of the best things to happen this year. We're happy to have you. I meant what I said at the back to school event. We hope you stay here for as long as we had Mrs. Magrady."

Nathan smiles. "Thanks, Erin."

"And do not ever scare me by giving your notice again," she says pointedly.

"Yes, ma'am."

"Good."

The first bell rings, signaling the start of the day.

"That's your cue. Have a great day, Mr. Woodson."

"You too, Principal Tanaka."

Nathan heads to his class when he runs into Greg.

"Hey. Were you just coming out of Erin's office?" Greg asks.

"Yep."

"Aw, man. I'm really sorry, Nathan. I heard about what happened at the bonfire. It was good to work with you."

"I didn't lose my job, Greg."

"What? How?"

Nathan motions for Greg to lean in. Greg gets closer.

"There is no rule about teachers and parents. We just can't do anything inappropriate on campus."

Greg takes in Nathan's words. "I guess this means I can start things up with Dana again."

"Greg, don't do it, man."

"I mean, one more time can't hurt."

The two of them laugh as Dana enters with Brad.

"Hi, Mr. Woodson," Brad says as he runs into the classroom.

"Hi, Brad."

Dana addresses Nathan. "Look, I'm sorry that you're going to lose your job. I shouldn't have told everyone what I saw."

Nathan looks at Greg, who is trying not to smirk. "I appreciate that, Ms. Kopel. But you have nothing to be worried about. I'm not leaving Glen Oak. Principal Tanaka didn't fire me."

"Does that mean parents and teachers actually can date?"

"It does," Nathan replies.

Dana looks at Greg with lust and focus.

"Friday night, Gregory. Be at my house by seven."

"Okay." Greg lowers his voice.

"I'll catch you later, Mr. Lucas," Dana says.

She walks away, victorious.

Greg looks at Nathan, defeated.

"You didn't even try to resist her," Nathan chastises his new friend.

"There was no point." Greg looks away in shame.

Nathan shakes his head. "Beers and burgers, Thursday after school?" Nathan grins.

"Can Katie come too?"

"Of course."

"Alright, see you at lunch."

Nathan smiles and heads into his classroom, ready to start the day.

Twenty-Eight

LATRICE

It's the end of the school year and things could not be better between Latrice and Nathan. He and Quincy have bonded like superglue. They have remained teacher and student in class, but once school ends next week, that's officially over. Meanwhile, Nathan and Quincy have been playing video games, watching movies and having in-depth discussions about the future of the MCU. Quincy and Eli even taught Nathan the secret handshake. For now, Quincy still calls him Mr. Woodson, but has said once school is over, he'll happily start calling him Nathan. On the last day of school, the plan is to have dinner at the taco spot by Nathan's old apartment just like he and Latrice talked about.

Nathan gave up his apartment in May and moved in with them. Latrice was worried about the adjustment at first, but she shouldn't have been. Nathan has been nothing but respectful of her and Quincy's space, and they have done everything to make him feel at home.

Latrice finishes getting ready. She has her hair styled in a sleek bun, and she's wearing a sleeveless cream-colored bandage dress with a deep V-neck and matching stilettos. Her makeup is minimal, with a simple eye shadow, mascara and a muted lip with gloss. Nathan is wearing a double-breasted cream-colored suit, with a brown tie and matching loafers.

"Look at us." Nathan smiles.

He stands behind Latrice as she puts some finishing touches on her makeup in the bathroom mirror.

"We do look good, don't we?"

"We look damn good, Lala."

Nathan kisses her bare shoulder. Latrice giggles as she feels tingles from the soft brush of his lips.

The two enter the living room and find Thad, Eli, Ashleigh and Quincy getting ready to watch a movie.

Thad lets out a whistle. "You two look sharp."

"Why, thank you." Latrice smiles.

"Thanks again for watching the kids, Thad," Nathan says.

"No problem. We're going to have some fun eating junk food and staying up late."

The kids eyes go wide, and they high-five each other.

Nathan leans over and whispers in Latrice's ear, "Twenty bucks says they're all out before the opening credits."

"Give them a little credit. They'll be out once the junk food wears off. I give them an hour," Latrice retorts.

They all say their goodbyes as Latrice and Nathan head out.

They enter Cork & Marble and are seated in the booth where they first met.

"Did you request we be seated here?" Latrice asks with a smile a mile wide.

"I might have." Nathan kisses her hand.

The waiter approaches their table and gets their drink orders.

Latrice gazes at Nathan and leans in to kiss his full, sweet lips.

"I love you so much, Nathan."

"I love you more, Latrice."

They kiss some more as the waiter returns and sets their drinks down.

"Are you two ready to order? Or do you need a few more minutes?"

"No need. We'll start off with the crab cakes. I'll have the ribeye, the lady will have the prime rib. Both cooked medium well. We'll both have the roasted potatoes and creamed spinach for sides, and we'll be splitting the berry and vanilla crème brûlée." Nathan hands him their menus.

"Very good. I'll put your order in." The waiter exits.

"I don't think I have ever been more turned on by you than I am now," Latrice says, gazing at him intently.

"I appreciate that, Lala, but I have to confess I looked at the menu online earlier so I'd know what to order. I wanted to make sure we actually ate something this time."

Latrice giggles. "Good plan."

They enjoy their meal, laugh, talk and feed each other. At the end of the evening, Latrice is eating the last spoonful of crème brûlée—at Nathan's insistence—when he pulls a ring box out of his pocket and places it on the table.

Latrice swallows her last bite and looks at it. "What's this?" she asks.

"My proposal." Nathan smirks.

He opens the box and slips a princess cut canary yellow engagement ring on her finger. Latrice looks down at it and smiles. Nathan's always telling her how good she looks in bright colors. She looks at the ring and is speechless. Her eyes fill with tears. When she looks back up at him, he has tears in his eyes. Taking her hand with the engagement ring, Nathan kisses it.

"Latrice Richardson, I've already told you this, but it bears repeating. From the moment I first laid eyes on you when you walked through that very door," Nathan points to the restaurant entrance, "I was enchanted and haven't stopped being enchanted every second we have been together. I know that you were unsure about us for various reasons, but I hope that you know that you are my forever. You are my everything. I could never fathom a life without you and Quincy in it. I want to be your husband and your best friend. I want to be everything to you. I want to be Quincy's stepfather. I want to continue being his teacher. I want to become his confidant, as well as his role model. I want to spend the rest of my life devoted to our family. I love you, Lala. Marry me." Nathan rubs the back of his hand against her cheek.

"Yes!" Latrice cries.

He pulls her to him and crashes his lips against hers. They kiss for an eternity.

The waiter clears his throat. When they don't stop, he clears it again. This time, he's louder. Latrice and Nathan look up at him.

"Sorry," they say in unison.

The waiter places the check on the table. "When you're ready—and from the looks of it, you both are—please let me know."

Within seconds, Nathan places his credit card into the leather check holder. The waiter happily takes it.

"Be right back." He tries to hold his laughter and walks away.

Nathan shrugs. "I'll leave him a good tip too."

They both laugh. Right as they're about to kiss each other again, the waiter reappears.

"You know, there's a hotel not that far from here," the waiter suggests.

"That's our next stop," Nathan replies.

Twenty minutes later, they enter the same room from the night they met.

"Did you seriously reserve everything from our first night together?"

"Sure did."

Waiting for them are a bottle of Moët and two champagne flutes. Nathan pours them each a drink and hands a flute to Latrice.

"Thank you."

"You're welcome."

They drink their champagne and look at each other hungrily. Nathan takes her glass and places the flutes on the nightstand. He pulls Latrice into his arms, kissing her. Reaching under her dress, he slips off her panties. He lifts her up, and she wraps her legs around his midsection before Nathan tosses Latrice onto the bed. She lets out a laugh when he leaps on top of her. She takes off his glasses and kisses him all over his face. The kisses turn into raw passion when she gets to his lips. Soon, they're practically ripping each other's clothes off. They stop long enough to stare at one another. Nathan rubs his hands on Latrice's breasts, and she lets out a sigh and kisses him along his jawline. No longer sneaking around and being able to love each other freely has her floating. A wide smile spreads across her face.

"What's that smile for, Lala?"

"I'm just so happy." She chokes up.

"Me too, baby. Me too. And I promise to keep making you happy for as long as I live."

"Nathan?"

"Yes."

"Remember when you said you were going to put a baby in me?"

"Yeah, I do."

"Well, what are you waiting for?"

Nathan chuckles. "What indeed?"

THE END

Acknowledgments

Thank you so much for reading "Hot for Teacher." I hope you enjoyed Latrice and Nathan's love story as much as I enjoyed writing it. I want to thank my husband Joe for all of his love and support and our children Michael and Alexander for being mommy's sweet little men.

I want to give a shout out to Leni Kauffman for her amazing work on the cover, Meka James for her top notch beta reading, Jessica Berry, one of the best editors in the business, Ian Moore for offering to sensitivity read the manuscript, Rae Shawn Love, the ultimate proofreader and Brynn who is my book formatter for life!

Stay tuned for Drea and Thad's story "Spend My Life with You." Coming in 2024.

www.ingramcontent.com/pod-product-compliance
Lightning Source LLC
Chambersburg PA
CBHW021802130726
47987CB00008B/2984